英译平果壮族嘹歌
——三月歌篇

陈　兵◎译

广西大学哲学社会科学文库

上海交通大学出版社
SHANGHAI JIAO TONG UNIVERSITY PRESS

内容提要

　　本书为平果壮族嘹歌《三月歌》的英译本。《三月歌》有相当长的篇幅描述人们观花、赏花、采花、插花、求花等与"花"相关的活动,因而又有人称其为"花歌"。《三月歌》共分十四部分,每部分采用汉英双语对照的模式呈现嘹歌的唱词。在优秀中华文化"走出去"的浪潮中,需要用文化翻译的方法对壮族嘹歌进行英译,以确保这份民间文艺瑰宝在保持本真性的基础上得到高质量的译介和对外传播。本书适合作为嘹歌爱好者传唱的歌本,也适合对非遗文化感兴趣的读者阅读。

图书在版编目(CIP)数据

　　英译平果壮族嘹歌. 三月歌篇: 中英对照／陈兵译
. —上海: 上海交通大学出版社,2022.7
　　ISBN 978 - 7 - 313 - 26946 - 1

　　Ⅰ. ①英… Ⅱ. ①陈… Ⅲ. ①壮族-民歌-平果县-
选集-汉、英 Ⅳ. ①I277.291.8

　　中国版本图书馆 CIP 数据核字(2022)第 103011 号

英译平果壮族嘹歌
──三月歌篇

YINGYI PINGGUO ZHUANGZU LIAOGE──SANYUEGE PIAN

译　　者:陈　兵
出版发行:上海交通大学出版社　　　地　　址:上海市番禺路 951 号
邮政编码:200030　　　　　　　　　电　　话:021 - 64071208
印　　制:江苏凤凰数码印务有限公司　经　　销:全国新华书店
开　　本:710 mm×1000 mm　1/16
字　　数:358 千字
版　　次:2022 年 7 月第 1 版　　　　印　　张:21
书　　号:ISBN 978 - 7 - 313 - 26946 - 1　印　　次:2022 年 7 月第 1 次印刷
定　　价:88.00 元

本书获得广西大学哲学社会科学文库资助出版

译 者 简 介

陈兵,女,广西大学外国语学院教授、硕士生导师;全国社科工作办同行评议专家,美国纽约州立大学人类学系高级访问学者(2015—2017)。曾主持完成国家社科西部项目一项(14XYY006);教育部人文社科规划项目一项(11YJA740003);获得广西第十三届社会科学优秀成果三等奖(201413322)。担任国内学术期刊《亚太跨学科翻译研究》常务副主编,澳大利亚亚太出版集团旗下的学术期刊《亚太人文与社会科学期刊》(*Asia-Pacific Journal of Humanities and Social Sciences*)编委。

序①

梁庭望

由罗汉田研究员壮文转写、汉文翻译的平果壮族嘹歌,包括《三月歌》《日歌》《路歌》《贼歌》和《房歌》五部民间长诗,共计 24 000 多行。这五部民间长诗,是根据广西平果县太平镇太平村布凌屯著名歌师谭绍明提供的民间传统抄本转写、翻译的。所谓"壮文转写",就是将用方块壮字(也称"古壮字"或"土俗字")手抄的壮族古籍转写为拼音壮文(也称"现代壮文")。

以口头形式和抄本形式相结合广泛流传于壮族民间的嘹歌,是壮族歌海里璀璨的明珠,是壮族文苑中艳丽的奇葩。它生长在广西平果、田东、马山、武鸣、大化一带右江河谷和红水河中游辽阔的壮乡大地上,以其悠久的历史、丰富的内容、深刻的内涵、别致的格式和高超的手法,一直受到人们的赞誉和青睐。如今,当你走到平果县城的公园里,无论是白天还是晚上,都会看到一群群、一组组自由组合的壮人,在如醉如痴地对唱嘹歌,那魅力绝对让你倾倒,不舍离去。

嘹歌成长到今天这样完美,并非一朝一夕之功,它是多少代壮族民间歌手和民间诗人用血汗和智慧浇灌而成的。它的完成虽然在明代,但从萌芽、发展到完善,无疑经过了漫长的岁月。在歌里,壮族庶民常常将自称"我"(gou)谦称为"奴"(hoiq),这是壮族奴隶制社会留给农奴制社会的遗韵。壮族的"奴"一共有三个词,一个是本民族词 hoiq(ho:i35),音"恢"。汉族进入岭南以后,又从汉语中借入"奴",音"挪"(noz,no31),后来又将 hoiq 与 noz 合成一个词 hoiqnoz。壮族进入奴隶制很早,广西武鸣县马头古墓群,最早的距今已经 3 100 多年,最晚的在战国初期,发掘表明,那时壮族社会已经产生阶级分化。

---

① 本书中文序和绪论选自《平果壮族嘹歌 三月歌篇》(民族出版社,2009 年)。歌书抄本由谭绍明提供,罗汉田进行壮文转写及汉文翻译。

到唐代,壮族奴隶制开始瓦解,逐步从奴隶制向封建农奴制转换。宋代农奴制确立,明代达到高峰,通称土司制。嘹歌用的是 hoiq 一词,这个词的产生当在秦统一岭南之前。这说明,嘹歌萌芽于先秦,经过漫长历史的不断充实、加工和扩展,日臻完善,最终完成于明代。明代壮族奴隶制虽然已经不存在,但庶民仍沿用"hoiq"作为谦称。由此可知,嘹歌从萌生到定型,至少历经了 2 000多年的历史。

壮族嘹歌的五部长诗,版本众多,各有所长。曾经出版过的版本,世人从中已经初步领略到她的风采。总的来说,她内容博大,蕴涵丰富,是明代右江及红水河中游一带壮族社会的百科全书,其中也包含明代以前的社会情状,故而有重要的艺术欣赏价值和历史研究价值。相对来说,壮文转写、汉文翻译的平果壮族嘹歌比较具有代表性,五部长诗都是民间歌师几十年前祖传下来的传统抄本。3 000 多行的《三月歌》,描绘两个小伙子去邻村寻找情人对歌的初步相识的过程,从对歌里,人们可以看到一年 4 个季节中每个季节的植物生长、动物情态和壮人的生产活动,其中对阳春三月的描绘极其生动,在这个季节里,春光绚丽,和风拂面,百草勃发,万物复苏,繁花似锦,新叶葱翠,一派生机盎然的生动景象。歌中给人们很多的生产生活知识,"Haeuxnaengj o/Gaem so bae conx deih/Conx deih aeu lwgmbwk/Daeuj dawz rug lawh meh"(糯饭乌/拿锄去整墓/整墓要女儿/来替娘守屋)这说明,早在明代以前,壮族就有三月初三蒸五色糯饭扫墓的风俗,而且女儿也要拿锄参加除草,给坟头添土,以示对祖先的感恩。《路歌》继上一部,描绘这对情侣相携出游的过程。他们穿过郁郁葱葱的森林和宽阔美丽的田野,一路问风、问水、问泉,赏风景,夸田园,叹身世,谈未来,充满了对幸福的憧憬。临别交换了信物,标志他们爱情的丰收。这首长诗的社会生活容量很大,他们把自己比喻为两只小野鸭、鱼鸟、白鲢、鳊鱼,在大自然中自由自在地生活。途中雷雨频仍,江河涨水,他们都像牛犊一样勇往直前,以此比喻其爱情经得起任何风浪的考验。从套七层衣服的描绘里,人们知道从前壮族的民族服装的多彩。《日歌》共 6 200 多行,描绘一对情人不期邂逅,他们在对歌中互相试探之后,双方直抒胸臆,倾诉爱慕之心,吐露眷恋之情,双双立下山盟海誓,决心冲破封建包办买卖婚姻藩篱,争取自由幸福美满的家庭生活,结婚以后,他们恩爱如故,相敬如宾,互相扶携,白头偕老,就是百年以后,仍也同过十座桥,同上一架梯,一起奔赴遥远的冥冥彼岸。整首长诗十分感人，完全可以说是一幅古代壮族社会生活、民族风情的生动画卷。4 000多行的《房歌》，实际隐喻爱情的归宿——构筑生活的空间，它全面而详细地咏唱了从商量建房、进山伐木、发墨开凿、买牛踩泥、打瓦烧砖、凿石安磉、合柱架梁、围墙砌砖到乔迁安神、赞房保宅等等干栏营建的全部过程。从中人们可以知道当时壮人居住的干栏其神龛是高低双层，高层安三香炉，点香烛，低层摆长条案，点长明灯；干栏有4排架、12主柱、26磉、120短柱、120枋、120檐，结构宏大，设备完整，光是水桶、水缸、水罐就各有几十对等等。其中虽然不乏艺术夸张，但规范的干栏规模及其设备，由此可见一斑。诗中提及的相关的信仰、禁忌、习俗、风情，更是生动具体，令人目不暇接。4 000多行的《贼歌》，和过去收集到的一些抄本内容大致相同，但只反映了土司之间的火并及其给老百姓造成的灾难，没有提到打八寨，兵锋北部只达到今马山县的乔利。其征调、惜别、行军、鏖战、归来、悔罪、重聚等过程，也与过去的版本略有不同。总而言之，嘹歌给后人留下了明代壮族社会的一个时代横断面，让后人从中走进前人斑斓多彩的生活，读后令人回味无穷。

嘹歌在艺术上有独特的韵味和鲜明的特色，其篇章结构、展开方式、描述手段、复沓方法，都既朴素而又精彩，引人入胜。中国少数民族的民间长诗类型比较多，主要分为创世史诗、英雄史诗、叙事长诗、抒情长诗、宗教经诗、哲理（伦理道德）长诗、历史长诗、信歌、套歌、文论长诗十种，壮族具备其中的九种，只缺乏文论长诗。这些长诗一般都独立存在，唯独嘹歌比较特殊，她将叙事长诗、抒情长诗、套歌有机地结合在一起，每部长诗都是按照一定的程序展开，其中的《三月歌》《日歌》《路歌》是按歌圩的套歌程序演绎的，《房歌》和《贼歌》则是按事情演化过程展开的，其程序都属于套歌。从局部上看，它们都有浓厚的抒情氛围，没有明显的连续的情节，属于抒情长诗。从整体上看，它们却是情节完整的叙事长诗。《贼歌》还融入了历史长诗的格局，叙述了一场土司之间为争权夺利而爆发的战争的整个过程。五部长诗的展开，与一般长诗按情节展开完全不同，情节的推进，都是通过男女对唱演绎的，其中有提问，有回答，有抒情，有叙事，有直述，有暗喻，有斗贫，有赞颂，形式活泼生动，语言诙谐有趣，完全打破了通常的时空排列，没有呆板的情节演绎，聆听咏唱让人自觉趣意盎然。其韵律以滚动式连环腰脚韵为主，其间插入四句式半"勒脚"韵，结构如下：

连环腰脚韵：

Song hoiq daengz gyaeuj giuz　　　　　（我俩到桥头）

　　　　　　　　A

Raen ga giuz senq raek　　　　　（见桥早已歪）

　　　A　　　B

Raen gij naek senq duenh　　　　　（见爱早已断）

　　　　　B　　　C

Naek senq duenh sam seiq　　　　　（断成四成三）

　　　　C

半"勒脚"韵：

Song hoiq bae caeg nduj　　　　　（我俩初上阵）

　　　　　　A

Bae cam youx aeu sai　　　　　（去问妹要带）

　　A　　　B

Baih de miz rumz lai　　　　　（那带风厉害）

　　　　　B

Cam aeu sai heux hwet　　　　　（问要带系腰）

　　　　B

这两种韵律婉转回环，得益于岭南的山回水转，有很强的音乐感。

嘹歌经过多少代民间艺人的加工，广泛使用复沓、借喻、明喻、暗喻、排比、借代等艺术手法，歌词优美精炼，有很强的艺术感染力。其中复沓使用最为普遍，如《三月歌》一首：

男：艳花开桥边，　　　　女：艳花开桥边，

　　鲜花浮河面。　　　　　　鲜花浮河面。

　　有船能观赏，　　　　　　无船去观赏，

　　无船空遗憾。　　　　　　看花流下滩。

男唱的四句歌词，以花借喻情人，又作起兴；以无渡船去观花喻没有办法得到情人的爱。女的答歌头两句，复沓男唱的头两句。嘹歌从头到尾普遍都是这样的结构，最少也复沓一句。这种复沓好处甚多，一是壮族对歌时要求对方歌声一停，自己的答歌马上还过去。如果是构思四句，是来不及的，一般听

完前两句,已经基本拟好后两句,可以迅速回应,否则会被耻笑为无能。二是嘹歌是唱给听众听的,复沓可以使听众听清歌词,便于理解。三是能够顺着对方的歌意准确地回过去,扣紧题旨,加深艺术感染力。在上面这首答歌里,女的就巧妙地将男唱的后两句稍作改变,即很好地回答:你如果不想办法,就只能眼睁睁地看花随水漂流而去,激将男方大胆追求。在嘹歌里,经常看到十问十答、二十四节气问答、渡十桥、十二月生产、打十闸等等这样结构相同的排比句型,使诗行活泼生趣。从艺术性来看,嘹歌在壮族民间长诗中是比较完美的。

为了尽量保持嘹歌完美的艺术风格,在壮文转写、汉文翻译中就不得不费尽心力。这首先归功于中共广西平果县委、县人大、县人民政府领导对优秀民族文化的理解和重视,他们在大力发展经济的同时,十分重视民族文化遗产的保护和民族文化品牌的打造。这说明,平果县领导对党中央关于民族文化的相关理论和政策的认识是比较到位的。在这场民族文化遗产保护和民族文化品牌打造的战役中,在前沿指挥的是县人大主任农敏坚。农敏坚同志对嘹歌的价值有深刻的理解,对相关的历史文化和民族风情相当熟习,繁忙的政务工作之中,他一直把嘹歌的搜集整理作为义不容辞的责任,并和其他领导同志一起,调度指挥,躬身实践,这才有嘹歌的转写、翻译。由于工作条件和生活条件都得到很好的安排,罗汉田才有一个全心投入转写、翻译的环境。翻译是两种语文的对接转换,由于两种语文的词语结构和表达习惯的差别,常常给翻译造成很大的障碍,其中的甘苦只有亲历才能品尝。罗汉田无疑经历了许多艰辛,克服了重重障碍,才得以将 24 000 多行的嘹歌转写、翻译完成。

转写、翻译的平果壮族嘹歌,其特点首先是选材典型,忠于原文,保存了嘹歌的原生形态,这一点最为重要。通观国内类似的翻译整理,往往得不到世界学术界的认可,究其原因就是对作品原生形态的任意剪接、任意增删和改变原义,把创作和收集混淆了。多年以后,人们才认识到保持民间作品原来真实面目的重要性。其次,要转写、翻译好嘹歌,对嘹歌词语的解读是最基本的工作,也是要突破的藩篱。好在右江土地是罗汉田的故乡,他是这块土地孕育出来的中国社会科学院研究员,由于他深谙这一带的民族语言,掌握民间用以记录这种语言的"土俗字",熟悉这一带的民族习俗风情,又得到多位著名歌师的指点帮助,因而对嘹歌词语及相关历史文化和风土民情的理解比较透彻,词语的壮文转写就比较准确,这为汉文翻译创造了比较坚实的基础。最后,汉译文比较准确流畅,忠于原文,不任意加减和曲解,较好地达到了翻译工作所要求的"信、达、雅"。原文的词语不添加,不随意解释,较好地处理对应关系,从而使译文的可信度大为提升。例如《三月歌》中的一首对歌:"今天真吉利/见喜鹊鼓翅/见鳄鱼呼风/见新人出门",原文是:"Ngoenzneix ndei yianz ndei/Raen roegciz dop fwed/raen dungieg siu rumz/raen lwg vunz ok moq",对译是:"今天好真好/见喜鹊鼓翅/见鳄鱼呼风/见儿他人出新",第二、三句完全对应,第一、四句虽然无法对应,但由于对原文理解比较准确,译文也就能够比较好地表达了原意。翻译比较完美还在于保持了原诗的音节结构,原诗是五言,译文也是五言,这样做虽然难度很大,但能够比较好地保持原文的诗性,不至于因为畏难而将诗体散文化,使诗意顿失。有些诗行难以对应,在译文后面加上注释,这不失为一种创新,能给读者自己琢磨的机会。例如《三月歌》中的一首:"二三月风大/落叶满山谷/山谷叶相混/满山白衣冒",末句原文是"mbauq daenj hau giet gyoengq",直译是:"美貌年轻人 穿白衣结成群",顺译是"穿白衣的美貌年轻人结成群",很难译为五言,故将"美貌年轻人"音译为"冒",并在句后注释:"mbauq:意为美貌年轻人,在此音译为冒,此句原义是穿白衣服的男青年结成群,在此译为满山白衣冒。"有这样的注释,对读者就很方便,也是译者忠于原文的相应措施。

总之,平果壮族嘹歌的转写、翻译本给我们带来了新意,虽然因为难度比较大,其中还有一些可以琢磨的地方,但终究是瑕不掩瑜。壮族民间诗歌浩如烟海,翻译出来的很少,令人满意的译本更少,平果壮族嘹歌可以说为壮族民歌译汉提供了一个新的范本,希望有更多的类似本子面世。是为序。

2008 年 5 月 2 日

于中央民族大学

Preface to *Pingguo Zhuang Liao Songs*[1]

Liang Tingwang

Pingguo Zhuang Liao Songs, transliterated from Zhuang language and translated into Chinese by Luo Hantian, the researcher of Chinese Academy of Social Sciences, consists of five long folk poems, including "Songs of March" "Songs of Day" "Songs of Road" "Songs of War" and "Songs of House", with a total of more than 24,000 lines. These five long folk songs are transliterated from the traditional folk manuscripts provided by Tan Shaoming, a famous singer from Bulingtun, Taiping Village, Taiping Town, Pingguo County, Guangxi. The so-called "Zhuang language transliteration" is to transliterate the hand-copied ancient books of the Zhuang ethnic group with Zhuang characters (also known as "ancient Zhuang characters" or "local folk characters") into Pinyin Zhuang characters (also known as "modern Zhuang characters").

Liao Songs, widely spread among Zhuang folk by combining oral form and transcription form, is a shining pearl in the sea of Zhuang songs and a gorgeous flower in the Zhuang literary garden. It has developed in Guangxi' Pingguo, Tiandong, Mashan, Wuming, and Dahua, the vast area of the Youjiang River Valley and the middle reaches of the Hongshui River with its long history, rich content, profound connotation, unique format and superb techniques, and has been praised and favored by Zhuang people for generations. Nowadays, when you go to the parks in Pingguo County, you will see groups of Zhuang people in free combination singing *Liao Songs* to each other ecstatically, day or night, whenever. The charm of *Liao Songs* absolutely fascinates you and makes you reluctant to leave.

So perfect that *Liao Songs* has been shaped and spread as what it is today, not overnight, but has been cultivated by many of Zhuang folk singers and folk poets with their blood, sweat and wisdom for generations. Although its completion was in the Ming Dynasty, it undoubtedly took a long time for it to undergo the process from germination, development to perfection. In *Liao Songs*, Zhuang plebeian people often called themselves "I" ("gou") humbly as "slave" ("hoiq"), which is the legacy of the serfdom society left by the slave society of the Zhuang ethnic group. The word "slave" of the Zhuang ethnic group has three characters, one is the national word "hoiq" (ho:i35), pronounced as "hui". After Han people entered Lingnan (South of the Five Ridges), they borrowed the word "slave" from Chinese, which sounds "noz" (noz, no31), then a new word "hoiqnoz" was formed by the combination of "hoiq" and "noz". Zhuang ethnic group entered the slavery society very early, and of the ancient Matou tombs in Wuming County, Guangxi, the earliest was more than 3,100 years ago, and the latest was in the early Warring States period, and the excavation showed that class division had already occurred in the Zhuang society at that time. In the Tang Dynasty, Zhuang slavery began to collapse, and gradually changed from slavery to feudal serfdom. Serfdom was established in the Song Dynasty and reached its peak in the Ming Dynasty, commonly known as chieftain system. *Liao Songs* uses the word "hoiq", which came into being before Emperor Qin unified Lingnan area. This shows that Liao Songs originated in the pre-Qin Dynasty. After a long history of continuous enrichment, improvement and expansion, *Liao Songs* became more and more perfect and was finally completed in the Ming Dynasty. Although slavery did not exist in the Zhuang nationality in the Ming Dynasty, the plebeian people still used "hoiq" as a modest title. Therefore, it could be concluded that *Liao Songs* has a history of at least 2,000 years from its birth to its finalization.

With five long poems *Liao Songs* of the Zhuang ethnic group has many editions and each has its own advantages. From the previous versions which had been published, the world has a preliminary appreciation of her elegant demeanor. Generally speaking, its content is broad and rich, and it is an encyclopedia of the Zhuang society in the middle reaches of Youjiang and Hongshui River in the Ming Dynasty, which also includes the social situation before the Ming Dynasty, so it has significant values both in artistic appreciation and historical research. Relatively speaking, *Pingguo Zhuang Liao Songs* transliterated from Zhuang language and translated into Chinese are quite representative, and the five long poems are all traditional manuscripts handed down by folk singers several decades ago. With more than 3,000 lines, "Songs of Lunar March" depicts the process of two young men going to a neighboring village to look for the young women they favored and singing in antiphonal style with them. From the vivid description of the songs, people can see the plant growing, animal breeding and the various production activities of Zhuang people in each of the 4 seasons of a year. The spring scenery is gorgeous, the breeze blows, the grass grows, all things revive, flowers bloom, and the new leaves are lush. What a lively and beautiful scene! The songs provide people a lot of knowledge about production and life. "Haeuxnaengj o/Gaem so bae conx deih/Conx deih aeu lwgmbwk/Daeuj dawz rug lawh meh" shows that as early as before the Ming Dynasty, Zhuang people had the custom of sweeping tombs with steamed five-color glutinous rice on the 3rd of lunar March, and the young girls participated in weeding and hoeing at the graves to show their gratitude to their ancestors. Following the "Song of March" "Songs of Road" describes the process of the couple mentioned above traveling together. They walked through the lush forests, and the broad and beautiful fields, asking about wind, water and springs, enjoying the scenery, praising the countryside, sighing out their lives, and talking about the future, full of longing for happiness. They exchanged gifts before their farewell, marking the harvest of their love. The long poem is rich in descriptions, in which the young couple compare themselves to two little wild ducks, fish birds, silver carps and mackerels, living freely in nature. There are frequent thunderstorms and river flooding on the way, and they both move forward as bravely as calves, which means that their love can stand the test of any storm. From the description of seven layers of clothes, people know the colorful ethnic costumes of the Zhuang ethnic group in the past.

"Songs of Day", with more than 6,200 lines, depicts two lovers who meet unexpectedly. After they sound each other out in singing the songs, they express their feelings and their love, and both make a vow of love and affection. They are determined to break through the barriers of feudal arranged marriage and strive for freedom, happiness and complete family life. After marriage, they love each other as usual, respect each other, help each other, grow old together, and even a hundied years passed, they still cross ten bridges together, go up the same ladder, and go to the distant heaven together. The whole long poem is a touching and vivid picture of the social life and ethnic customs of the ancient Zhuang ethnic group.

The more than 4,000 lines of "Songs of House" actually symbolize the destination of love — building the space of life. It depicts comprehensively and in details the process of building a stilted house, from discussing building a house, cutting trees in the mountains, carving ink and digging, buying cattle for stepping on the mud for foundation, burning tiles and bricks, chiseling stones, building beams, bricklaying walls, to keeping housewarming activities, praising and protecting the houses, and so on. From which people can know that the structure of the stilted house that Zhuang people lived in at that time was a double-layer one, with three incense burners on the high layer, incense candles on the lower layer, long strips on the lower floor, and ever-burning lanterns on the lower floor; the stilted house had 4 rows of shelves, 12 main columns, 26 piers, 120 short columns, 120 square-columns and 120 eaves, with a grand structure and complete equipment, which include dozens of pairs of buckets, same number of tanks and pots. Although there is some artistic exaggeration, the standard scale of the stilted house and its equipment can be seen from the above description. The relevant beliefs, taboos, customs and practices mentioned in the poem are more vivid, concrete and dizzying.

The more than 4,000 lines of "Songs of Wars" are roughly the same as some manuscripts collected in the past, but they only reflect the fight between chieftains and the disasters they have caused to the common people. "Songs of War" does not mention the battle in Bazhai, and the forces only reach Qiaoli in the north which is now Mashan County. The process of requisition, farewell, march, fierce battle, return, repentance and reunion is also slightly different from the past version. In a word, *Liao Songs* has left a cross-sectional picture of Zhuang society in the Ming Dynasty, which makes future generations feel the colorful life of their predecessors after reading.

Liao Songs has unique charm and distinctive features in art. Its structure, ways of unfolding, means of description, rhetoric technique of repetition are plain yet fascinating. There are many types of long folk poems of ethnic groups in China, including creation epics, heroic epics, long narrative poems, long lyric poems, religious classics poems, philosophical (ethical and moral) poems, historical poems, letter songs, set songs, and literary theory poems. Among which, the Zhuang ethnic group has nine of them, and only lacks literary theory poems. Usually, these long poems exist independently, but *Liao Songs* distinguishes itself with the others by combining long narrative poems, long lyric poems and set songs organically, developing each of its five long poems with certain procedures. Among them, "Songs of March" "Songs of Day" "Songs of Road" are performed in accordance with the set song program of the song fair, while "Songs of House" and "Songs of War" are unfolded according to the development of the stories. Both types belong to the set songs. Taken as a part, they all have a strong lyric atmosphere without obvious continuous plots, so they belong to long lyric poems. However, taken as a whole, they are long narrative poems with complete plots. Integrated with the pattern of a long historical poem, "Songs of War" depicts the process of a war between chieftains for the sake of power and fortune. Totally different from the general long poems which develop according to the plots, the five poems unfold its plots via singing in antiphonal style between man and woman, in which questions and answers, lyricism and narratives, narration and metaphor, bicker and praise are interwoven with each other. The form is active and lively, the language is witty and interesting, completely breaking the usual arrangement of time and space. There is no rigid plot interpretation, thus, listening to the singing of *Liao Songs* makes people feel intrigued. Its rhythm is mainly based on rolling the interlinking foot-waist rhyme, with four and half sentences inserted for iterative rhyme. The structure is as follows:

Interlinking Foot-Waist Rhyme:
　　We arrive at the bridge
　　　　　　　　A
　　Seeing the bridge was broken.
　　　　　　A　　　　B
　　Love has broken for long
　　　　　　B　　　C
　　Into pieces we don't want.
　　　　　　　　　C

Semi Iterative Rhyme
　　The first time we meet
　　　　　　　　A
　　Sister gives me my girdle
　　　　　　A　　B
　　Over there strong winds blow
　　　　　　　　B
　　Ask for girdle to tie waist
　　　　　　B

These two rhythms turn back gracefully, with a strong sense of music, thanks to the turning of mountains and rivers in Lingnan area. After being processed by folk artists for many generations, *Liao Songs* have widely adopted the artistic techniques such as repetition, metonymy, simile, metaphor, parallelism, metonymy, etc., showing beautiful and refined lyrics and strong artistic appeal. Among them, repetition is the most popular way which has been frequently used in *Liao Songs*; take one poem from "Songs of Luner March" as example:

Male:

By bridge pretty flowers bloom,

On river fresh flowers float.

Available to watch with a boat,

Or we regret back home

Female:

By bridge pretty flowers bloom,

On river fresh flowers float.

No a boat to watch,

Beach flowers flow beneath.

The four lines of lyrics sung by the male starts to use flowers as metaphors for his lover, which act as the prelude; to watch flowers without a boat means that he can't get the love of his lovers. The first two lines of the female sung repeat the first two lines of the male singer, which is the general framework frequently seen in *Liao Songs*, at least one line is repeated in the female's lyrics. This kind of repetition has many advantages. Firstly, when the Zhuang people sing in antiphonal style, the female singer is required to immediately answer her counterpart's singing once he pauses. Usually it's too late for her to compose four lines, and generally, after listening to the first two lines, the female singer has basically drawn up the last two lines so that she could respond antiphonally and swiftly, or she will be ridiculed as incompetent. Secondly, *Liao Songs* are sung for the audience, repetition can make the audience hear the lyrics clearly and easy to understand. Thirdly, it is able to follow the counterpart's meaning, not only to accurately make the musical dialogue go smoothly, but also to focus on the theme so as to broaden the artistic appeal. In the above mentioned answer song, the female cleverly changes the last two lines of the male singer, that is, she answers the male very well: if you can not figure out a solution to the problem, you will end up watching the flowers drift away with water. In this way she actually intends to encourage the man to pursue her boldly. In *Liao Songs*, we often see ten questions and ten answers, questions and answers on 24 solar terms, crossing ten bridges, production of December, hitting ten gates, and so on, which make the lines lively and interesting. From an artistic point of view, *Liao Songs* are relatively perfect in the long folk poems of the Zhuang ethnic group.

In order to keep the perfect artistic style of *Liao Songs*, great efforts have been made in Zhuang transliteration and Chinese translation. First of all, this is attributed to the understanding and attention towards the excellent ethnic culture from the leaders of the Party Committee, People's Congress and People's Government of Pingguo County. While developing the local economy, the Pingguo County administration has attached great importance to the protection of ethnic cultural heritage and the building of ethnic cultural brands, which shows that the leaders of Pingguo County all levels have fully comprehended the relevant theories and policies of the CPC Central Committee on national culture. Among them, Nong Minjian, the director of Pingguo People's Congress, is in command at the forefront. He has a considerable insight of the value of *Liao Songs*, and is quite familiar with the relevant history, culture and ethnic customs. In his busy administrative work, he has always regarded the collection and arrangement of *Liao Songs* as his obligatory duty, and takes a lead in organizing and managing the team for the transliteration and translation of *Liao Songs*. Pleasant working and living conditions are provided to Luo Hantian, so that he could concentrate his mind on transliteration and translation. Translation is the connection and transformation of two different languages. Due to the sharp differences in word structures and expression habits between the two languages, usually great obstacles have occured in translation, in which the pleasure and hardship can only be tasted through personal experience. It is without doubt that Luo Hantian has cracked all kinds of obstacles before he was able to transliterate and translate *Liao Songs* with more than 24,000 lines.

Authenticity is the priority of selecting the typical material and keeping it faithful to the original *Liao Songs* in transliteration and translation. Literature reviews show that similar domestic translation and arrangement are usually not recognized by the international academic circle, for its arbitrary editing, adding, deleting and changing the original meaning of the lyrics, etc., thus confusing the boundary between creation and collection in the preservation of *Liao Songs*. It takes a long time for people to realize the significance of authenticity in keeping the folk works.

Secondly, in order to transliterate and translate *Liao Songs*, the interpretation of the words is the most basic work, and the first barrier to break through as well. Fortunately, Youjiang River Basin is the hometown of Luo Hantian, in which he was born and cultivated to be a trained researcher of the Chinese Academy of Social Sciences. Being familiar with the local dialects, and the vernacular characters which are applied in recording folklore as well, knowing well the ethnic customs in this area, and guided and instructed by many famous singers of Liao Songs, Luo Hantian has acquired a panoramic view on *Liao Songs* and its related background of history, culture and customs. Therefore, his transliteration of words in Zhuang language is more accurate, which creates a relatively solid foundation for Chinese translation.

Thirdly, his Chinese translation is accurate and fluent, faithful to the original, without arbitrary addition, subtraction and misinterpretation, thus has achieved the criteria of "faithfulness, expressiveness and elegance" in the translation of poems. The words in the original text are neither being added nor being deducted, nor are they being interpreted at will, and the corresponding relations are handled properly, so that the credibility of the translation is greatly improved. Take a piece of duet songs in "Songs of Lunar March" as an example, in which the lyric in Zhuang language goes like this: "Ngoenzneix ndei yianz ndei/raen roegciz dop fwed/raen dungieg siu rumz/ raen lwg vunz ok moq". The original translation is: "What a good day/see the magpie spread its wings/see the crocodile call the wind/see others bring forth the new". When it comes to English translation, it goes like this: "What a good day today, magpie its wings to display, flood dragons whistling in water, out the newlyweds to play". The second and the third sentences correspond with each other exactly, although the first and the fourth sentences cannot correspond, but due to the accurate understanding of the original text, the Chinese translation can better express the original meaning in Zhuang language. The better translation also lies in maintaining the syllable structure of the original poem, which is composed of five characters in a line, and the translations of each line also keep in five characters. Although it is very difficult to do so, it can better maintain the poetic nature of the original text, so as not to scatter the poetic style and lose the poetic flavor because of the hardship in poem translation. Some lines are difficult to correspond to, so adding notes after the translation can be regarded as a kind of innovation and can give readers a chance to ponder it for themselves. Take another piece of duet songs in "Songs of Lunar March" as an example, in which the lyric in Zhuang language goes like this: "Ngeih sam nyied rumz hung/mbae fung loenq laj lueg/loenq laj lueg dox gyaux/mbauq daenj hau giet gyoengq". The literal translation of "mbauq daenj hau giet gyoengq" is "handsome young men wear white clothes and they come in groups". Its transliteration is "groups of handsome young people dressed in white", which is hard to translate into five characters in a line, so it is wise to translate the phrase "handsome young people" into "Mao", with a note to explain the meaning of "mbauq" in Zhuang language and its culture, and the poem's English translation is "February and March it is windy, maple leaves are in valley, various leaves all are mixed, crowds of boys are in white". With such notes, it is very convenient for the reader to understand the meaning of the lyrics of *Liao Songs*, and it is also a corresponding measure for the translator to be faithful to the original text.

In a word, the transliteration and translation of the *Pingguo Zhuang Liao Songs* have brought us new ideas, and although there are still some places that need to be improved due to the difficulties involved, its successful transliteration and translation are well worth appreciation. There are hundreds and thousands of Zhuang folk poetry, yet few have been translated into Chinese, and even fewer satisfactory translations. *Pingguo Zhuang Liao Songs* can be said to have provided a new model for the translation of Zhuang folk songs, and I'm looking forward to the publication of more similar books. The above serves as the preface.

2008 – 05 – 02

in Minzu University of China

绪　论

罗汉田

1

在广西壮族自治区右江中游北岸、红水河中游南岸的平果、田东、马山、大化、武鸣等县壮族地区，流行一种壮语称为"吩嘹"（Fwen liuz）的双声部民歌。"吩"（Fwen）汉意为民歌；"嘹"（liuz）是这种民歌的称谓，"吩嘹"（Fwen liuz）汉意即"嘹歌"。

关于"嘹歌"的含义，大体来说有五种说法：

（1）这种民歌多由上、下两个乐句组成，每一个乐句末尾，都带有一声长约四拍"嘹—嘹—"的衬词拖音，因此人们称这种民歌为"嘹歌"，即"带有'嘹'衬词的歌"。

（2）在壮文里，"嘹"（liuz）这个词汇其汉意是"流传"，因为这种民歌流传历史相当悠久，流传范围相当广泛，因此人们便称之为"吩嘹"，即"广泛流传的歌"。

（3）在壮文里，"嘹"这个词其音接近于"料"（liuh），"料"（liuh）的汉意是"游玩""娱乐"，因此人们称这种游玩时大家娱乐所唱的歌为"吩嘹"，即"游玩娱乐的歌"。

（4）右江北岸平果、田东毗连的这一带地方是"嘹歌"主要传唱地，这一带的壮人自称"僚"（liuz），其居地称"那僚"，"僚"与"嘹"同音，"嘹歌"就是"那僚人唱的歌"。

（5）历史上壮族先民他称为"僚"，"散居山谷"的"僚"人能歌善唱，所唱的歌人们称之为"僚歌"，如今的"嘹歌"，正是历史上传承下来的"僚歌"，即"僚人所唱的歌"。

以上五种说法，前面四种来自民间，最后一种出自学者。不论是来自民间,还是出自学者,所有的这些说法,都有它的道理,也都持之有据,并能自圆其说。不过,民间的那四种比较通俗的说法,似乎更接近于事实,因而更容易被人们接受,被人们认可。

2

"嘹歌"这种双声部壮族民歌,曲调相当丰富。仅在平果一县境内,就有"哈嘹""那海嘹""嘶咯嘹""长嘹""迪咯嘹""哟咿嘹"等七八种。这些曲调,旋律悠扬,风格各异,共同组成了异彩纷呈的"嘹歌"音乐。这些被人们誉为"天籁之音"的"嘹歌"音乐,长期以来一直受到不少音乐工作者的青睐,被他们采录作为音乐教学的教材和音乐创作的素材。2006 年由广西电视台选送参加第十二届全国青年歌手大奖赛并闯入决赛、由"平果嘹歌组合"四位壮族姑娘演唱的《百年嘹歌唱春天》(农敏坚作词、傅磬作曲)、《木棉树下两相依》(农礼生编曲)等歌曲以及广东著名作曲家马国华先生最近创作的《盛世嘹歌》《阿妹唱嘹歌》《我们一起唱嘹歌》等数首歌曲,就是以流行于平果县海城乡一带的"那海嘹"和流行于太平镇一带的"哈嘹"为素材创作的。广西平果铝业公司"哈嘹乐团"几个年轻的业余歌手演唱并被录制成 CD 大量发行的《月亮》《山中画眉》《故乡》等脍炙人口的歌曲,也是以现代摇滚音乐和传统"嘹歌"音乐相结合创作和演唱的既具有现代气息又有民族传统的时尚歌曲。这些让人感到耳目一新、受到不同年龄层次听众欢迎的歌曲,很难说它们不是"嘹歌"音乐的最新发展,更难说它们不是"嘹歌"音乐今后发展的一个方向。

"嘹歌"的唱词,大体来说分有两种,一种是触景生情、即兴编唱,另一种相对来说比较固定。这种相对来说比较固定的唱词,在民间,男性歌手一般都有用"土俗字"(壮语称 saw ndip)传抄的歌本。这些用"嘹歌"曲调演唱的比较固定的唱词,以及用"土俗字"记录、传抄这些固定唱词的歌本,人们称之为嘹歌。传统的嘹歌歌本,大部分是本地出产、手工制作、韧性很好的棉纸,其大小一般只有两三个指头那么宽,一个多指头那么长。抄写时,有的把整句唱词五个字全部抄写,也有的只抄写每一句唱词的头两三个字甚至只抄写头一个字,而且一般只抄写男方的唱词而不抄写女方的唱词。因此,民间流传的嘹歌抄本,绝大部分都是只有"男歌"而没有"女歌"。对歌时,由其中的一位男歌手掌握歌本,两位歌手一边看着歌本一边引吭高歌,女歌手则根据男歌手所唱的内容接唱对答。所答的唱词,也是基本固定,世代传承,原辙复蹈,少有变易。也就是说,"嘹歌"流传地区男女歌手所对唱的嘹歌,一般来说都是墨守成规,有"书"为证。即使稍有变化,那也是不越雷池,不离其宗。

3

根据民间歌手唱歌或抄歌的习惯,嘹歌包括"日歌"和"夜歌"两大部分。"日歌"即白天唱的歌,主要由《三月歌》和《日歌》两部长歌组成。

《三月歌》的内容是,初春时节,风和日丽,百花盛开,生意盎然,两对男女青年结伴来到青山脚、泉水边、树荫下、花丛中,一边采鲜花、摘春笋、拾野菜,一边猜谜语、讲笑话、对情歌。一场春雨沥沥降下,潺潺流水注入稻田,紧张繁忙的春耕季节来到了。人们纷纷赶回家里整理犁耙,运送肥料,播种育秧。热烈愉快的劳动,更加激起人们歌唱的热情,人们一边劳动一边歌唱,一直唱到来年的正月十五。

《日歌》这部长歌描述一对分别被父母包办结婚的中年男女在趁圩路上不期而遇,于是双方互相对歌,表白胸臆,倾吐爱情。不料事情暴露,男女双方不仅受到非议,而且遭到家人辱骂,甚至被送官问罪,戴枷游街。但是,所有的这些并改变不了他们追求婚姻自由的初衷。他们不屈不挠地与家庭、与官府作顽强的抗争,甚至不惜倾家荡产,卖牛赎身,终于得以结合成为眷属。

《夜歌》即夜晚唱的歌,主要由《路歌》《贼歌》《房歌》三部长歌组成。

《路歌》又称《行路歌》,是一部生活气息十分浓郁的抒情诗,是历史上壮族人民"倚歌择偶"婚恋习俗的真实写照,是壮族男女青年谈情说爱的传统歌经。长歌以一群男女青年结伴出游走村串寨为线索,一路之上,大家将路上所见所闻以歌代言互相酬唱。酬唱当中,他们亦步亦歌,触景生情,以情驭景,以景显情,描述十分形象生动,比喻尤其贴切新鲜。最后,男女双方情投意合,大家互相赠送信物,并且立下山盟海誓。

《贼歌》叙述一对热恋中的青年男女正在忙着备办嫁妆,突然风云骤变狼烟骤起,各地土司四处调兵征战,男青年也在被征调之列。分别之时,虽然依依难舍,但因头人逼迫,只好挥泪惜别。连日行军到达前线,时值春夏之交,终日阴雨绵绵,敌对双方在深山峡谷连日鏖战。正当打得死去活来雄雌不分时,土官突然下令偃旗息鼓,丢甲弃械,仓皇还乡。还乡路上,无粮无饷,米珠薪桂,为了活命,男主人公只得典去身上衣,卖掉头上帽,换取筒把米,以求得一饱,经历万般辛苦诸多曲折,终于保住性命回到家乡,与久别的恋人重新团聚。

《房歌》包括"建房"和"褒房"两个部分,也是通过男女对唱的形式,贯穿以青年男女别致的恋情彩线,将壮族群众建房盖屋活动中从伐木、备料、踩泥、打砖、烧窑、安磉、立柱、上梁、架檩、盖瓦直至踩门、入居、安灶、贺房、保宅等等营造过程以及材料长短尺寸、房屋开间宽窄、室内空间划分、家具陈设配置和各种各样祭祀仪式、相关习俗风情等等作详细的描述,表达了人们追求居家平安、家代昌盛的美好愿望。

总的来说,平常人们所说的"嘹歌",实际上包含着它的曲调部分和它的唱词部分,即音乐部分和文学部分。如果我们形象地将"壮族嘹歌"这个名词比喻为一瓶酒,那么,酒瓶就是它的音乐部分"嘹歌",而它的文学部分就是这个酒瓶里面的佳酿。像人们看中一瓶酒不仅因为看中精美的酒瓶同时也看中瓶中之美酒一样,"嘹歌"之所以受到人们的高度重视,不仅是因为它优美动听的旋律,同时也是因为它博大精深的内容和精彩生动的唱词。也就是说,"嘹歌"的价值不仅体现在它的音乐部分,同时也体现在它的文学部分。其文学部分是壮族文学史乃至中国文学史上占据重要地位的民间文学作品,是壮族文化宝库中璀璨夺目的绚丽明珠。

4

作为壮族文化宝库璀璨明珠的嘹歌,艺术性最高、思想性最强、最具有文学价值和史料价值的,是其中的《贼歌》这一部长歌。

在《贼歌》这一部长歌里,有"调去打贼蛮""调去打贼乙""调去打贼猛"等唱词,还多次提到"乔利"这一地名,有军旗"一面跟一面/齐奔乔利坡""今刚到那楞/明又奔乔利""乔利四天路/合做一天赶"和"哥出征回来/快马过乔利"等唱词。

从长歌的内容来看,唱词中提到的"贼蛮""贼乙""贼猛",显然就是李蛮、黄骥和岑猛这三个历史人物,而"乔利"这个地方,就是明正统六年(1441年)至嘉靖七年(1528年)思恩土府府衙所在地。曾经把李蛮、黄骥、岑猛这三个人物和乔利这个地方联系起来的,是闻名于史的"思田之乱"。

明成化十九年(1483年),田州(今广西田阳县地)土知府岑溥与其侄恩城

（今广西平果县榜圩镇地）土知州岑钦相互攻伐，岑溥败走，岑钦攻入田州，大肆烧杀。弘治三年（1490 年），岑钦再次攻伐田州，与泗城（今广西凌云县地）土知府岑应相勾结，二人分据田州。弘治五年（1492 年），岑钦杀害岑应父子，不久，岑钦父子又被岑应之弟岑接杀死。岑钦死后，岑溥重返田州，但又于弘治十二年（1499 年）被其长子岑猇所弑，随后岑猇亦自杀。土目黄骥企图独揽田州大权，与兵总李蛮发生冲突。黄骥挟持岑溥才四岁的次子岑猛投奔思恩知府（府治今马山县乔利镇）岑濬，向岑濬贿以重赂并献其女，又许诺割划田州之六甲等地，于是岑濬支持黄骥，调兵助他对付李蛮，派员护送岑猛返回田州，但是李蛮仍不允许岑猛进城，岑猛只好重又暂居思恩。后来，在中央王朝的干预下和岑濬的威逼下，岑猛才得返回田州袭土知府职。此后，岑濬乘机向岑猛勒索分地，不料遭到岑猛拒绝。岑濬达不到占夺领地的目的，便联合泗城土知府岑接和东兰土知州韦祖鋐，各自起兵攻打李蛮，相约分占田州土地。《明史》载："韦祖鋐率兵五千助思恩岑濬攻田州，杀掠男女八百余人，驱之溺水死者无算"；岑接率兵二万攻入田州后，"括府库，放兵大掠""杀掠万计，城廓为圩"；岑濬则"率兵二万攻旧田州，据之，杀掠男女五千三百余人"。

在此之前，岑濬自成化十六年（1480 年）承袭思恩土知府职后，便"筑石城于丹良庄，屯兵千余人，截江以括商利"；又"筑周安堡"，"以头目黎瑞率兵屯守"，自恃强雄多次兴兵四出掳掠独霸一方。岑濬的行径不仅造成生灵涂炭民不聊生，也直接危及中央王朝对桂西地区的封建统治，于是，弘治十八年（1505 年），省总潘蕃、太监韦经、总兵毛锐奉命调集广西、湖广官军及土司兵丁共十万八千人，兵分六哨讨伐岑濬。岑濬虽然"分兵阻险拒敌"，但终抵挡不住"官军奋勇直前"，只好退守老窝兴宁。官军继续围攻，岑濬无路可逃，最后自刎兴宁城内。至此，"思恩遂平"，其代价是"斩捕四千七百九十级，俘男女八百"。

就这样，自成化至弘治这二十多年间，桂西一带一直处在土司之间争权夺利和中央王朝征调用兵的战乱之中。这场战乱，很可能就是《贼歌》最直接的历史背景，是民间歌手把这场战乱作为作品情节的基干或主体，通过一对经历悲欢离合的壮族青年男女发自内心的对唱，从一个侧面愤怒控诉这场旷日持久的不义战争给桂西一带人民群众带来的深重灾难。由此可以推断，嘹歌中的《贼歌》这一部长歌，其雏形当形成于"思田之乱"以后不久，即距今四百多年的明代中后期。这个年代的推断，应该是嘹歌形成、产生的最低下限，而其上限则因为缺乏确凿的证据而难以断定。不过，根据《三月歌》《路歌》和《日歌》所叙述的一些内容、所描绘的一些习俗、所反映的一些生活和所透露的一些信息等等来看，其上限很可能至少是在唐宋时期甚至更早之前。

5

根据实地考察，唐宋时期甚至更早之前传唱至今的嘹歌，其传唱地域与当年的思恩土州、府所辖范围相当一致。

思恩土府的前身是始建置于唐乾元元年(758 年)的羁縻思恩州，州署在今平果县旧城乡兴宁街。元代，思恩州废。北宋皇佑四年(1052 年)，浙江余姚人岑仲淑随宋王朝枢密副史狄青依智高，功晋金紫禄大将、沿边溪峒军民安抚使，管辖邕州(今南宁)。仲淑死后，其子岑自亭袭职，不久被诬谋反，被迫退出邕州，迁至乔利。传至岑世兴一代，归附元朝，王朝加封为总兵万户侯，故而阿谀奉承，以其子改用元人名氏。世兴临终，将封地一划为四分其四子，三子阿兰次得乔利，为思恩土官始祖。传至岑永昌，已是明代。洪武八年(1376 年)，永昌将州署迁回故地(今平果县旧城镇兴宁街)。永乐十八年(1420 年)，永昌之子岑瓛死无后嗣，时年 27 岁的岑瑛以“官弟”身份继袭，成为思恩土州第四代州知。

岑瑛继袭之后，由于他有谋略，有才干，勤政为民，治理有方，减轻税赋，免除征调，百姓一度得到休养生息，辖境之内比较平稳安定，农业生产获得较大发展，加上他对朱明王朝心诚悦服，与朱明王朝始终保持一致，故而得到朱明王朝赏识，官职爵位一再晋升，多次得到封疆赐地，短短几年时间，便使思恩州由一个只有三百来户人家的小土州很快就扩大、升迁为拥有近三千户人家的军民府。正统七年(1442 年)，岑瑛将思恩府治迁至乔利，但今旧城乡兴宁街仍为思恩土州治所，岑瑛仍掌州事。岑氏家族在乔利思恩土府经历了岑瑛、岑鐩、岑濬三代，至嘉靖七年(1528 年)王守仁率兵镇压八寨壮瑶农民起义之后，才把思恩土府改为思恩军民府并将衙署迁至武缘的荒田驿(今武鸣县府城镇)，又将思恩府折建兴隆、白山、定罗、安定、古零、旧城、那马、下旺、都阳九个土巡检司。

自明永乐十八年(1420 年)继袭至成化十四年(1478 年)寿终，岑瑛前后在位执掌州府事长达 58 年。期间，他除了“以山为城，石垒其缺”，修筑兴宁山城,并分别亲题"兴宁""悦服"楷体大字于对峙峭壁之外,还非常重视辖境之内的文化教育和文化建设,大力提倡创建学宫,极力鼓励学习儒学。《明史》卷318记载,正统十二年(1447年),明王朝就曾应思恩土知府岑瑛之请,在思恩"设儒学,置教授一员,训导四员"。景泰五年(1454年),明王朝又"从瑛请,建庙学"。而他本人不仅"崇儒敬道",而且以身作则,十分"好学",以至"积为满家"。所有的这些,无论是对其家族后代,或者是对其他姓氏土司,均产生很大影响。

由于岑瑛倡立学宫,召民入学,首倡思恩读书风尚,营造良好文化氛围,因此,思恩州、府治所在的兴宁,便于无形之中形成了一个文化中心;思恩州、府所辖的这片地域,也于无形之中形成了一个独具特色的文化圈,并在文化圈形成的过程当中不断向外辐射,向外扩展,不断巩固和提升自身的地位。

地位不断巩固、不断提升的一个重要标志,是一个为数不少的土司家族诗人群体的层出涌现。以思恩府辖地丹良堡一地为例,明清两代数百年间,以王受(原为思恩州所辖丹良堡土目,后授白山土巡检司巡检世袭)的老家、今太平乡袍烈村贯屯为基点繁衍的王氏家族,就先后涌现出十几位颇有造诣的用汉文写作的文人,他们互相酬唱,共同切磋,创作了数量相当可观的诗文作品。在贯屯附近的山上,至今仍可看到他们多处的题诗石刻。他们的诗歌作品除了结集付梓流传于世,还有五位诗人的十几首诗作被《三管英灵集》《粤西诗载》等历史上颇有影响的诗集收录,成为弥足珍贵的文化遗产。

这样一种浓厚的文化氛围,正是嘹歌孕育、产生的腴沃土壤;吮吸着民族文化充足养份的嘹歌这棵幼苗,正是在这样一片钟灵毓秀热土之上茁壮成长,日臻成熟,馨香袭人。也就是说,有明一代的思恩土州府以及以后的下旺巡检司、旧城巡检司和丹良堡飞地所管辖的这一片地域,正是嘹歌孕育、产生、形成、发展、逐步规范并广泛流传的核心地域。而嘹歌里所提及的一些地名,以及目前嘹歌仍然盛行的地域,也从多个角度客观地证实了这一点。

6

目前仍然广泛流行的嘹歌,20世纪50年代初期就受到民间文艺工作者的关注。从1955年起,当时在田东县文化馆工作的黄耀光先生就开始从事《贼歌》的搜集。1961年广西民间文学研究会("广西民间文艺家协会"前身)成立后不久,也组织专家深入田东、平果进行调查,搜集新的资料。1963年,广西民间文艺研究会和田东县文化馆共同搜集的嘹歌中之《贼歌》,由已故著名民间文艺家黄勇刹先生和黄耀光先生翻译、整理后,以《唱离乱》为题发表于当年的《广西文艺》第5期。1980年,《唱离乱》被收入上海文艺出版社出版的《中国民间长诗选》第二集。

1986年广西少数民族古籍整理出版规划领导小组暨办公室成立后,又将嘹歌的搜集、整理、翻译、出版纳入广西少数民族古籍整理出版规划,作为《壮族民歌古籍集成》之一于1993年由广西民族出版社出版。在这之前,广西民族出版社还于1985年出版了由莫非等人搜集的壮文版《三月歌》《大路歌》《离乱歌》《建房歌》和《献歌》。

1994年,中华人民共和国文化部与联合国教科文组织签订了旨在保护中国民间口承文学遗产的"项目实际计划协议书";2000年12月,又签署了旨在保存中国少数民族民间歌谣和口述传说的"行动计划"协议。根据这两份协议的精神,2003年1月12日,由中国民间文艺家协会组织、有中国社会科学院专家参加的采录小组在广西南丹县里湖乡结束了对白裤瑶祭祀古歌的采录之后,即转至田东,用了整整一天的时间,在田东县思林镇与平果县太平镇毗连的"坎仰"(岩洞名),从头至尾完整地对嘹歌中的《贼歌》进行实地采录。中国社会科学院民族文学研究所研究员罗汉田根据实地采录的音像资料用壮文转写、汉文翻译的《贼歌》文本除了交存于联合国教科文组织总部,2007年5月又被中央民族大学"'985工程'中国少数民族语言文化教育边疆史地研究创新基地文库"收入"中国少数民族非物质文化研究系列",作为"中国少数民族口承文学资料丛编"由民族出版社出版。

在此之前和在此之后,平果县的民间文艺工作者对广泛流传于平果本地的壮族嘹歌也非常重视。早在20世纪60年代初期,时为民办小学教师后来历任中学校长、中共平果县委常委、县委统战部长、县人大副主任等职的李修琅先生就对嘹歌怀有浓厚兴趣,并动手搜集到嘹歌5部长歌的多种抄本。李修琅先生的嘹歌抄本,大部分都是在歌圩上搜集到的。据调查,20世纪60年代初期,平果县境内的传统"嘹歌"歌圩共有18个,80年代以后,保持唱歌活动的有12个。在这12个歌圩上,不同年代不同"版本"的嘹歌抄本随地可见,随手可得,有的还专门抄写销售于市。最近几年,原平果县城关乡教办室副主任黄国观先生就在不同歌圩上搜集到 30 多本不同年代、不同"版本"的嘹歌抄本。为了让这些嘹歌民间抄本能够保存下来、传播出去,2004 年,平果县人民政府调集了一定的人力、花费了一定的时间、动用了一定的经费,在县人大常委会主任农敏坚先生主持下,对搜集到的嘹歌抄本经壮文转写、翻译整理以后,由广西民族出版社以《平果嘹歌》为名正式出版,并于 2005 年 9 月 26 日在广西艺术学院演播礼堂举行"嘹歌飞扬——壮族歌圩音乐展示会暨壮族民歌文化丛书《平果嘹歌》首发式"。广西民族出版社出版的这一部篇幅浩瀚、内容繁复的《平果嘹歌》,分《长歌集》《恋歌集》《散歌集》《客歌集》《新歌集》5 大卷,共约 600 万字。与此同时,还配套出版了约 20 万字的《嘹歌嘹亮》论文集。由于平果县人民政府一方面从非物质文化遗产这一角度不断加大力度对嘹歌(文学部分)加以保护,一方面将天籁之音"嘹歌"(音乐部分)作为平果县的文化品牌加以打造,因此,近几年来,越来越多不同学科的专家学者纷纷将目光转移到平果,聚焦平果这片文化内涵深厚的沃土,聚焦至今仍然活存于这片沃土的奇葩。

"壮族嘹歌"这朵奇葩将旺盛活存,直到永远。

"壮族嘹歌"这朵奇葩将永不凋谢,馨香四溢。

Introduction

Luo Hantian

1

On the north bank of the middle reaches of the Youjiang River in Guangxi Zhuang Autonomous Region, among the Zhuang ethnic group areas of Pingguo, Tiandong, Mashan, Dahua, Wuming and other counties on the south bank of the middle reaches of the Hongshui River, there is a popular duet folk songs called "Fen Liao" (Fwen liuz in Zhuang language). "Fen" (Fwen) means "folk songs" in Chinese; "Liao" (liuz) is the title of this kind of folk songs, and "Fen Liao" (Fwen liuz) means "Liao Songs" in Chinese.

Generally speaking, there are five important points in "Liao Songs":

(1) This kind of folk song is mostly composed of upper and lower phrases, and at the end of each line, there is a dragging sound with a lining word about four beats long, so people call this kind of folk song "Liao Song", that is, "song with the lining word of 'Liao' ".

(2) In Zhuang language, the Chinese meaning of the word "(liuz)" is "spread", because this kind of folk songs has a long history and spread widely, so people call it "Fen Liao", which means "widely spread songs".

(3) In Zhuang language, the pronounciation of the word "Liao" is close to that of "Liuh". The Chinese meaning of "liuh" means "playing games" or "entertainment". Therefore, people call the songs sung in entertainment as "Fen Liao", which means "songs for playing and entertainment".

(4) The area adjacent to Pingguo and Tiandong on the north bank of Youjiang River is the main region where "Liao Songs" are sung. The Zhuang

people in this area call themselves "Liuz", and their residence is called "Na Liuz". "Liuz" and "Liao" have the same pronunciation, and "Liao Songs" are "the songs sung by Liuz".

(5) In history, the ancestors of the Zhuang ethnic group were called "Liuz". The "Liuz" who lived in the valley were good at singing, and the songs they sang were called "Liuz songs". Today's "Liao Songs" are precisely the "Liuz Songs" inherited from the ancient Zhuang people. That is, "the songs sung by Liuz".

Of the above five sayings, the first four come from the folk and the last one from scholars. Whether it comes from the folk or from scholars, all these sayings have their own reasons, in which they can hold the water with sufficient evidences. However, the four popular folklores seem to be closer to the truth, so they are more easily accepted by people.

2

"Liao Songs" are duet Zhuang folk songs with rich tunes. In Pingguo County, there are seven or eight kinds of tunes, such as Fwenhajleux(哈嘹), Fwenrungh(长嘹), Fwennazhaj(那海嘹), Fwendigw(底格嘹), Fwenswjgoz (斯格嘹), Fwenyoyi(哟咿嘹), and so on. With different melodies and styles, these tunes gradually have formed "Liao Songs", which are known as "the Sound of Nature", have been favored by many musicians for a long time, and have been collected as teaching materials for music teaching and music creation. In 2006, Guangxi TV Station selected singers to participate in the 12th National Young Singers Grand Prix, "Singing Spring for Hundred Years " sung by four Zhuang girls from "Pingguo Liao Song Group" (Nong Minjian wrote the lyrics and Fu Qing composed the music) reached the final; songs such as "Together Forever under the Kapok Tree" (composed by Nong Lisheng), as well as the "Liao Songs at Flourishing Age", "Sister Singing Liao Songs" and "Together We Sing Liao Songs" recently created by Mr. Ma Guohua, a famous composer of Guangdong Province are all based on "Nahai

Liao", which is popular in the area of Haicheng, Pingguo County and "Ha Liao", which is popular in Taiping Town. Several young amateur singers from Guangxi Pingguo Aluminum Company have set up a band called "Ha Liao Band", and have sung and recorded into CD many popular songs such as "Moon" "Mountain Thrush" and "Hometown". They are also fashion songs with modern flavor and ethnic tradition created and sung by the combination of modern rock music and traditional "Liao Song" music. It is difficult to say that these songs, which are refreshing and welcomed by listeners of different ages, are not the latest development of "Liao Songs", let alone a direction of the future development of "Liao Songs".

Generally speaking, there are two kinds of lyrics in "Liao Songs", one is impromptu compiling and singing evoked by the scene which brings back old memeries; while the other is relatively fixed. This relatively fixed libretto, in the folk, male singers generally use songbooks copied in "vernacular characters" (in Zhuang language, it is called "saw ndip"). These relatively fixed lyrics sung in "Liao Song" tunes, and the songbooks in which these fixed lyrics are recorded and copied with "vernacular characters" are called "Liao Songs". Most of the traditional songbooks are locally produced, handmade with resilient cotton paper, and are usually two or three fingers wide and about one finger long. Some copied all the five characters in a line, some copied only the first two or three characters, or even the first character, and they generally copied only the man's lyrics, not the woman's. Therefore, most of the manuscripts of Liao Songs circulated among the folk are "male songs" but not "female songs". When singing to each other, one of the male singers holds the songbook, and the two singers sing loudly according to the songbook, while the female singer sings in antiphonal style according to what the male singer has sung. The lyrics answered are also basically fixed, handed down from generation to generation, following the same track without any changes. In other words, "Liao Songs" spread in the area where male and female singers sing in antiphonal style generally follow the rules, centering on the songbooks.

It is obvious that Liao Songs remain essentially the same despite all apparent changes.

3

According to the habit of singing or copying songs by folk singers, "Liao Songs" include two parts: "Day Songs" and "Night Songs". Day Songs are the songs sung during the day, mainly composed of "Songs of March" and "Day Songs".

"Songs of Lunar March" depicts the sceneries in early spring, when breeze blows and the flowers are in full bloom, two couples of young men and women come together at the foot of mountain, the edge of the spring, the shade of trees, and the clusters of flowers, picking flowers, bamboo shoots and wild vegetables while guessing riddles, telling jokes, and singing love songs in antiphonal style. Spring rains fall, gurgling water flows into the rice fields, and the busy spring ploughing season is coming. People rush back home to arrange ploughs and rakes, transport fertilizers, sow and raise seedlings. Happy work in the field has aroused people's enthusiasm for singing, and people sing songs while working, until the 15th day of the first lunar month in the coming year.

The long song "Day Songs" describes a middle-aged man and a middle-aged woman who got married arranged by their parents respectively and met unexpectedly on the way to the folk song fair, so they sang in antiphonal style, expressed their feelings and love to each other. Unfortunately, their secvet love was exposed and both the man and the woman were not only criticized, but also abused by their family members, and they were even condemned by the feudal official, and were paraded along the streets with fetters. However, all these sufferings could not change their original wish of pursuing freedom of marriage. They fought tenaciously with their families and the local government, even at the expense of all their possessions, selling cattle to redeem themselves, and the lovers finally got married.

"Night Songs" is the song sung at night, which is mainly composed of "Songs of Road" "Songs of Wars" and "Songs of House".

"Songs of Road", also known as "Walking Songs", is a lyric poem with a strong flavor of life, a true portrayal of the love and marriage custom which Zhuang people inherited from their ancestors of "choosing a spouse according to singing songs" in history. "Songs of Road" is a traditional song for young men and women of the Zhuang ethnic group when they are courting each other. This long song depicts a group of young men and women who travel around the village, with everyone singing songs on what they have seen and heard along the way. In the antiphonal singing, they express their emotions in singing songs whenever they are touched by the scenes they've seen, and the descriptions delivered with the rhetoric techniques of metaphor are vivid and lively. Finally, the man and woman fall in love with each other, and they give each other the gifts and make vows of eternal love.

"Songs of War" tells the story of a young man and a young woman in love who are busy preparing a wedding when the situation suddenly changes, and warning signals of the approaching enemy forces are seen on all sides. Conscription is universal as the chieftains lauch the war. The young man is among them. At the time of parting, although he was reluctant to go for the war, he has to bid farewell in tears with his fiancée owing to the order for war from the tribal chief. They march on to the front day and night, and as it is at the turn of spring and summer, it is rainy all day long, while the opposing sides are fighting fiercely in the deep mountains and valleys. Just at the critical moment when both sides are fighting fiercely against each other, the local official suddenly order his army to stop fighting and throw away their arms and return home in a panic. On the way back to his hometown, there is no food, no pay, and price is high while life is difficult. In order to survive, the man has to pawn his coat and hat in exchange for a barrel of rice for food. After thousands of hardships and many twists and turns, he finally saves his life and returns home, and he is reunited with his long-lost lover.

"Songs of House" includes two parts: "Building House" and "Commending House". It displays the theme of love between the young men and the young women via the songs singing in antiphonal style. In the building activities of the Zhuang people, from logging, preparing materials, stepping on mud, beating bricks, firing kilns, founding piers, columns, upper beams, frames and tiles, covering tiles to stepping on doors, entering the stove, greeting houses, protecting houses, etc., as well as the length and size of materials, the width and height of houses, the division of interior space, furniture furnishings and various sacrificial ceremonies and related customs are described in details in "Songs of House". It shows the good wishes of Zhuang people to pursue peace at home and prosperity of the family generation.

Generally speaking, "Liao Songs" which people usually call actually consists of its melodies and lyrics, that is, its music and literature. If we vividly compare the term "Liao Songs of Zhuang ethnic group" to a bottle of wine, then the wine bottle is its musical part of "Liao Songs", and its literature part of *Liao Songs* is the fine wine in this bottle. Just as people take a fancy to a bottle of wine not only because of the exquisite wine bottle, but also because of the fine wine in the bottle, "Liao Songs" is highly valued by Zhuang people, not only because of its beautiful melody, but also because of its broad and profound content and wonderful and vivid lyrics. In other words, the value of Liao Song is reflected both in its music part, and in its literature part. The literary part of *Liao Songs* is an important folk literature work in the history of Zhuang literature and even Chinese literature, and it is a dazzling pearl in the treasure house of Zhuang culture.

4

Liao Songs is a shining pearl in the treasure house of Zhuang culture, of which, the long song "Songs of War" has the highest artistry, the strongest thought, and the most literary value and historical data value.

In this long poem "Songs of War", there are lyrics such as "transfer to fight Bandit Man" "transfer to fight Bandit Yi" "transfer to fight Bandit Meng" and so on. The place name "Qiaoli" has been mentioned for many times. There are lyrics such as military flag "running to Qiaolipo one by one" "just arriving at Naleng/running to Qiaoli again tomorrow" "Qiaoli's four-day journey/working together for a day" and "brother going back from battle/ quickly passing Qiaoli".

Judging from the content of the long poem, "Bandit Man" "Bandit Yi" and "Bandit Meng" mentioned in the lyrics are obviously the three historical figures Li Man, Huang Ji and Cen Meng, and the place "Qiao Li" is the location of Si'en government office from the 6th year of the reign of Emperor Zhengtong (1441) to the 7 year of the reign of Emperor Jiajing (1528) in the Ming Dynasty. What has associated the three characters Li Man, Huang Ji and Cen Meng with the place of Qiaoli, is the well-known "Rebellion of Sitian" in history.

In the 19th year of the reign of Emperor Chenghua in the Ming Dynasty (1483), Cen Pu, the local magistrate of Tianzhou (now Tianyang County, Guangxi), fought Cen Qin, his nephew, and also the local magistrate of Encheng (now the town of Bangxu, Pingguo County, Guangxi). Cen Pu was defeated, and Cen Qin invaded and destroyed Tianzhou. In the 3rd year of the reign of Emperor Hongzhi (1490), Cen Qin attacked Tianzhou again, and did evil things in collusion with Cen Ying, the local magistrate of Sicheng (now Lingyun County, Guangxi), and they divided Tianzhou into several parts and administrated them seperately. In the 5th year of the reign of Emperor Hongzhi (1492), Cen Qin killed Cen Ying and his son. Soon after, Cen Qin and his son were killed by Cen Ying's younger brother Cen Jie. After Cen Qin's death, Cen Pu returned to Tianzhou, but was killed by his eldest son Cen Xiao in the 12th year of the reign of Emperor Hongzhi (1499), who also committed suicide afterwards. Huang Ji, the local magistrate attempted to monopolize the power over Tianzhou and fought with Li Man, the general commander of his troop. Huang Ji hijacked Cen Pu's four-year-old second son Cen Meng to the local government of Sien (now in Qiaoli Town, Mashan County), bribed Cen Jun and offered his daughter to him, and promised him to cut off the top six pieces of lands in Tianzhou to him, so Cen Jun supported Huang Ji with soldiers from his troops to fight against Li Man, and sent officers to escort Cen Meng back to Tianzhou, but Li Man still did not allow Cen Meng to enter the city, and Cen Meng had to stay in Si'en for the time being. Later, under the intervention of the central government and the threat from Cen Jun, Cen Meng could return to Tianzhou to succeed his father as the local magistrate. Since then, Cen Jun took the opportunity to extort land from Cen Meng, only to be rejected by Cen Meng. Cen Jun could not achieve the purpose of seizing the territory, so he joined with Cen Jie, the local magistrate of Sicheng County, and Wei Zuhong, the local magistrate of Donglan County, and respectively attacked Li Man and they agreed to occupy the land of Tianzhou together. According to the history of the Ming Dynasty, "Wei Zuhong led 5,000 soldiers to help Cen Jun, the local magistrate of Si'en to attack Tianzhou, killing and looting more than 800 men and women, not including the drowning victims who were driven out". Cen Jie led 20,000 troops to storm into Tianzhou, who "opened the treasury house, and let his troops to rob anything they saw", and "killed and plundered thousands of people, and the city wall was totally destroyed". Cen Jun "led 20,000 soldiers to attack the old Tianzhou town, more than 5,300 men and women were killed in this battle".

Prior to this, after Cen Jun inherited the post of the local magistrate of Si'en from the 16th year of the reign of Emperor Chenghua (1480), he "built a stone city in Danliangzhuang, assembled an army of more than a thousand men, intercepted the river for commercial profits", "built Zhou'an Castle to be stationed with soldiers led by Li Rui", and sent his strong army force to plunder and dominate the other counties nearby". Cen Jun's behavior not only caused misery of people, but also directly endangered the feudal rule of the central government over western Guangxi. Therefore, in the 18th year of the reign of Emperor Hongzhi (1505), provincial general Pan Fan, eunuch Wei Jing and general commander Mao Rui were ordered to mobilize a total of 108,000 Guangxi, Huguang and chieftain soldiers, who were divided into six branches to fight against Cen Jun. Although Cen Jun "divided his troops to block and resist the enemy", he finally could not resist "the official troops marching forward courageously", so he had no choice but to retreat to Xingning, his base. Official troops continued to besiege Xingning, so Cen Jun had no way to escape, and finally he had to kill himself in the city of Xingning. At this point, the price of "quelling the rebels of Si'en" is "killing 4,790 people and capturing 800 men and women".

In this way, for more than 20 years from Chenghua to Hongzhi, the area of western Guangxi was in a war between chieftains fighting for power and interests, the constant recruitment of troops by the central government to quell the rebels. This war is probably the most direct historical background of the "Songs of War" which is regarded by folk singers as the main theme of the creation of this Liao Song, in which a young man and a young woman who experienced joys and sorrows, complained about the disaster that this protracted unjust war has brought to Zhuang people in western Guangxi through antiphonal singing. It can be assumed that the "Songs of War" in *Liao Songs* was formed shortly after the "Rebellion of Sitian", that is, more than 400 years ago in the mid and late Ming Dynasty. The inference of this era should be the lowest limit for the formation and production of *Liao Songs*, while its upper limit is difficult to determine because of the lack of conclusive evidence. However, according to some of the contents described, some customs described, some life reflected and some information revealed in "Songs of March" "Songs of Road" and "Day Songs", the upper limit is likely to be at least before the Tang and Song dynasties or even earlier.

5

According to the on-the-spot investigation, the region that *Liao Songs* was sung in the Tang and Song dynasties or even earlier is quite consistent with the scope of the Si'en local prefecture and its government at that time.

The predecessor of Sien prefecture was Jimi Si'en prefecture which was founded in the first year of the reign of Emperor Qianyuan in Tang dynasty (758 A.D.). The prefecture office is located in Xingning Street, the old town of Pingguo County. In Yuan Dynasty, Si'en prefecture was abandoned. In the 4th year of the reign of Emperor Huangyou of the Northern Song Dynasty (1052), Cen Zhongshu, a native of Yuyao, Zhejiang Province, followed Di Qing, the Song Dynasty's pivotal deputy secretary, and Nong Zhigao, the Senior General of Jin Zi Lu, and the chief military and civilian officer of Yanbian Xidong as well, to administrate Yongzhou (now Nanning). After Zhongshu's death, his son Cen Ziting succeeded to the throne, and was soon framed that he conspired against the state, so he was forced to withdraw from Yongzhou and move to Qiaoli. In the generation of Cen Shixing, they submitted to the authority of Yuan goverment, and was appointed as the commander in chief in a fief of 10-thousand-households. For flattery, he changed his son's name to the name of Yuan people. On his deathbed, Shixing divided his fief into four for his four sons, and the third son, Alanci, got Qiaoli, and was regarded as the first Si'en local magistrate. It was passed on to Cen Yongchang in the Ming Dynasty. In the 8th year of the reign of Emperor Hongwu (1376), Yongchang moved the state office back to its old place (now Xingning Street, an old town in Pingguo County). In the 18th year of the reign of Emperor Yongle (1420), Cen Huan, the son of Yongchang, died without an heir, and Cen Ying succeeded him in the capacity of "official's brother" and became the fourth-generation governor of Si'en prefecture.

After Cen Ying's succession, owing to his strategies, talents and diligence in governance (i. e. reduced taxes and tariffs, exemption from levy and transfer), the local people could be recuperated, the jurisdiction was relatively stable, and agricultural production developed greatly. Besides, he was loyal and obedient to the Ming government, and kept consistent with the

Emperor Zhu of Ming Dynasty, so he was appreciated by the central government, and his was promoted to higher ranks again and again, and he was also granted land several times in just a few years. As a result, Si'en prefecture quickly expanded and was promoted from a small local prefecture with only about 300 households to a military and civilian government with nearly 3,000 households. In the 7th year of the reign of Emperor Zhengtong (1442), Cen Ying moved the Si'en prefecture to Qiaoli, but then Xingning Street in the old urban and rural areas was administrated by the state, Cen Ying was in charge of state affairs. The Cen family experienced three generations of Cen Ying, Cen Sui and Cen Jun in the Si'en prefecture of Qiaoli. In the 7th year of the reign of Emperor Jiajing (1528), after Wang Shouren led troops to suppress the uprising of the Bazhai Zhuang Yao peasants, the Cen family changed the Si'en prefecture into Si'en military and civilian government, and moved it to Huangtian post in Wuyuan (now Wuming County), and divided the Si'en prefecture into nine branches: Xinglong, Baishan, Dingluo, Anding, Guling, Old City, Nama, Xiawang, and Duyang.

From Cen Ying's succession as the local magistrate in the 18th year of the reign of Emperor Yongle in Ming Dynasty (1420), to his death in the 14th year of the reign of Emperor Chenghua (1478), Cen Ying was in charge of the state capital for as long as 58 years. During this period, in addition to "taking the mountain as the city and building the stone foundation for its deficiency", he built the mountain city of Xingning, and wrote the characters of "Xingning" and "heartfelt admiration" in regular script on the two cliffs opposite each other; he also attached great importance to the cultural education and cultural construction within his jurisdiction, vigorously advocated the establishment of a school, and strongly encouraged the study of Confucianism. Volume 318 of the *History of the Ming Dynasty* recorded that in the 12th year of the reign of Emperor Zhengtong (1447), in response to the invitation of Cen Ying, the magistrate of Si'en, the Ming government had appointed "one professor and four tutors for teaching Confucianism". In the

5th year of the reign of Emperor Jingtai（1454）, the Ming government approved Cen Ying's proposal to "construct temples for Confucian learning". On the other hand, Cen Ying himself not only "worships Confucianism and Taoism", but also set a good example for the others, and he was so "studious" in learning that he "accumulated all these virtues for his whole family". All of these had a great impact on the descendants of his family and on other groups of magistrates as well at that time.

As Cen Ying advocated the school education, summoned the local people to study at school, initiated the fashion of learning is Si'en and created a good cultural atmosphere, Xingning, the capital of Si'en prefecture, gradually became a cultural center. This area under the jurisdiction of Si'en prefecture and the local government also virtually formed a unique cultural circle, and in the process of the formation, it continued to radiate and expand outward, and constantly consolidated and enhanced its own status.

An important sign of the continuous consolidation and improvement of this area was the emergence of a large number of chieftain family poets. Taking the Danliangbao, a place under the jurisdiction of Si'en prefecture as an example, during several hundred years of the Ming and Qing dynasties, the hometown of Wang Shou（originally the Danliangbao chieftain under the jurisdiction of Si'en prefecture, later being granted the Baishan Patrol Inspection Department hereditary inspector）, where his family flourished, is now called Guantun in Paolie village, Taiping town. Guantun successively brought forth more than a dozen accomplished literati who wrote in Chinese, who sang and learned from each other, and created a considerable number of poetry and prose works. In the mountains near Guantun, many of their poems engraved in stone carvings can still be seen today. In addition to their poems collected and published in the world, more than a dozen poems written by five of the poets have been collected into the influential collections such as *Sanguan Poetic Collections* and *Yuexi Poems* , which have been regarded as the precious cultural heritage of Guangxi.

Such a strong cultural atmosphere is fertile soil where *Liao Songs* is nurtured and produced; the seedling of *Liao Songs*, which has absorbed the sufficient nourishment of ethnic culture, has thrived and matured day by day on such a land, which is full of nature bestows, rich in historical cultural resources and natural resources. In other words, this area was under the jurisdiction of the Si'en prefecture of the Ming Dynasty and later the Xiawang Patrol Department, the Old City Patrol Department and the Danliangbao enclave. It is the core area where *Liao Songs* has been conceived, produced, formed, developed, gradually standardized and widely spread. Some of the place names mentioned in *Liao Songs*, as well as the areas where *Liao Songs* is still popular at present, have objectively confirmed this point from many perspectives.

6

Liao Song is still widely popular at present, has attracted the attention of folk writers and artists since the early 1950s. Mr. Huang Yaoguang, who worked in the Tiandong County Cultural Center at that time, has been engaged in the collection of "Songs of Wars" since 1955. Shortly after the establishment of the Guangxi Folk Literature Research Association (the predecessor of the Guangxi Folk Literature and Art Association) in 1961, experts from different disciplines were also organized to make on-the-spot investigation in Tiandong and Pingguo to collect new material. In 1963, the "Songs of War" in *Liao Songs*, which was jointly collected by Guangxi Folk Literature and Art Research Association and Tiandong County Cultural Center, was translated and sorted out by the late famous folk writers Huang Yongcha and Huang Yaoguang. The essay entitled with "Songs of Turmoil of War" was published in the 5th issue of *Guangxi Literature and Art* that year. And in 1980, it was included in the second episode of *Selected Chinese Folk Poems* published by Shanghai Literature and Art Publishing House.

After the founding of Guangxi Leading Group and Office of Planning for

Collation and Publication of Ancient Books of Ethnic Minorities in 1986, the collection, arrangement, translation and publication of *Liao Songs* were incorporated into the Guangxi Minority Ancient Books Arrangement and Publishing Plan. As one of the "Collections of Ancient Books of Zhuang Folk Songs", it was published by Guangxi Ethnic Publishing House in 1993. Prior to this, Guangxi Ethnic Publishing House published the Zhuang version of "Songs of March" "Songs of Road" "Songs of War" "Songs of House" and "Songs of Dedication" collected by Meng Fei and his collegues in 1985.

In 1994, the Culture Ministry of the People's Republic of China and the Educational, Scientific and Cultural Organization of the United Nations signed the Agreement on the Practical Plan for the Protection of Chinese Folk Oral Literary Heritage in December 2000, and an Agreement on the Action Plan for the Preservation of Chinese Minority Folk Songs and Oral Legends was also signed. According to the two agreements, on January 12, 2003, a team organized by the Chinese Folk Artists Association which included experts from the Chinese Academy of Social Sciences collected and recorded the ancient sacrificial songs of Bai Ku Yao minority in Lihu town, Nandan County, Guangxi. Then they transferred to Tiandong County and spent a whole day in the "Kanyang" (the name of a cave) which was adjacent to Silin town, Tiandong county and Taiping town, Pingguo county to make on-the-spot recording of the "Songs of War" in *Liao Songs* from the very beginning to the end. Luo Hantian, a researcher at the Institute of Ethnic Literature of the Chinese Academy of Social Sciences, based on the audio-video materials collected on the spot, finished his transliteration from Zhuang language, and Chinese translation of the lyrics of "Songs of War", the Chinese version of which has been kept at the headquarters of UNESCO. In May 2007, it was also collected by the Archives of Chinese Minority Language, Culture and Education Frontier History and Geography Research Base funded by Minzu University of China "985 Project", as a series of oral literature materials of Chinese ethnic minorities in Chinese Minority Intangible Culture Research

Series, and was published by the Ethnic Publishing House.

Before and after this, folk writers and artists of Pingguo County also attached great importance to the *Liao Songs* of the Zhuang ethnic group, which were widely spread in Pingguo. Early in 1960s, Mr. Li Xiulang, who was a teacher of a civilian-run primary school and later served as the principal of a middle school, a member of the standing Committee of the Pingguo County CPC Committee, director of the United Front Work of the County Party Committee, and deputy director of the County People's Congress, had a strong interest in *Liao Songs*, and he began to collect a variety of transcripts of the Liao Songs. Most of the transcripts of Liao Songs obtained by Mr. Li Xiulang were collected at the song fair. According to the survey, in the early 1960s, there were 18 traditional Liao Song fairs in Pingguo County, and 12 fairs have still kept singing activities since the 1980s, in which transcripts of Liao Songs of different ages and versions can be found, and some of them are specially copied and sold in the market. In recent years, Mr. Huang Guoguan, former deputy director of the teaching office of Chengguan town, Pingguo County, has collected more than 30 transcripts of Liao Songs from different ages and different versions at different song fairs. In order to enable these folk transcripts of Liao Songs to be preserved and popularized, in 2004, the People's Government of Pingguo County mobilized a certain amount of manpower, spent a certain amount of time and used certain funds. Under the leadership of Mr. Nong Minjian, chairman of the Standing Committee of the Pingguo County People's Congress, the transcripts of Liao Songs, after being collected, were transcribed, transliterateted from Zhuang language and then translated into Chinese, and were officially published by Guangxi Ethnic Publishing House with the title *Pingguo Liao Songs*. On September 26, 2005, "Liao Songs Flying — Zhuang Song Fair Music Exhibition and the First Publication Ceremony of Zhuang Folk Song Culture Series" was held in the Performance Auditorium of Guangxi Academy of Arts. Vast in length and complicated in content, *Pingguo Liao Songs* series published by Guangxi

Ethnic Publishing House, are divided into five volumes: Long Song Collection, Love Song Collection, Prose Song Collection, Guest Song Collection, and New Song Collection, with a total of about 6 million Chinese characters. At the same time, a collection of essays entitled "Loud Liao Songs", which is about 200,000 Chinese characters, has been published. On the one hand, the People's Government of Pingguo County has made more and more efforts to protect *Liao Songs* (literary part) from the perspective of intangible cultural heritage. On the one hand, it is cultivating "Liao Songs" (music part) — the sound of nature and turning it into a cultural brand of Pingguo County. Therefore, in recent years, more and more experts and scholars from different disciplines have turned their attention to Pingguo, focusing on Pingguo, a fertile soil with profound cultural connotations and the wonderful literary and artistic works that still exist.

May the wonderful work of Zhuang Liao Songs live exuberantly forever.

May the wonderful work of Zhuang Liao Songs never fade and its fragrance be overflowing forever.

目录 | Contents

三 月 歌

  《三月歌》这首长歌属于日歌,但也有人把它当作夜歌来唱。也就是说,这首长歌对唱的场合相对来说比较自由,对唱时间、对唱地点均没有十分严格的规定和限制。其中的"建月歌""时辰歌"和"水旱歌"这三节,又可以从中分离出来当作三首相对独立的短歌,穿插于日歌和夜歌对唱过程的间隙,作为日歌和夜歌对唱过程中的"调味品"。

  从内容方面来看,这一首长歌有相当长的篇幅描述人们观花、赏花、采花、插花、求花等等与"花"相关的活动,因而又有的人称这一首长歌为 Fwen va,汉译为《花歌》。

  原歌不作分段,为便于阅读,根据长歌内容大体分为若干段落。

Songs[1] of Lunar March

  "Songs of March" is a long song, which belongs to the day song, but some people sing it as a night song. In other words, the occasion of duet singing of this long song is relatively free, and there are no very strict regulations and restrictions on time and place. The three sections of this long song, namely "Jianyue Song" "Hour Song" and "Flood and Drought Song" can be separated as three relatively independent short songs, interspersed between day songs and night songs as a "condiment" in the process of duet singing.

  In terms of content, this long song has devoted much space to describe people's activities related to "flowers", such as viewing flowers, appreciating flowers, picking flowers, arranging flowers, asking for flowers. So some people name this long song as "Fwen Va" (Zhuang language pronounciation)[2], which is translated into Chinese as "Songs of Flowers".

  The original song is not sectionalized, but for readers' convenience, it is divided into several parts according to the content.

相逢 Meeting First

男： 今天真吉利
Male： What a good day today

见喜鹊鼓翅
Magpie its wings to display

见鳄鱼³呼风
The ngieng summon the wind

见新人出门
Out the newlyweds to play

女： 今天真吉利
Female： What a good day today

见喜鹊鼓翅
Magpie its wings to display

见鳄鱼呼风
The ngieng summon the wind

见春风扑面
On face spring breeze blows

男： 今天是吉日
Male： What a good day today

见画眉欢歌
Thrush sings songs all day

见了哥[4]讲话
Daeggo speaking over the trees

见友人出游
Hustle bustle the villagers make

女： 今天是吉日
Female： What a good day today

见画眉欢歌
Thrush sings songs all day

见了哥讲话
Daeggo[5] speaking over the trees

大家都出游
Out most of villagers to play

男： 大家都出游
Male： Out most of villagers to play

从上游到下
From the upstream to bottom

那位像情妹
Who is my favorite sister

玉立屋檐下

Under eaves she stands grace

女： 大家都出游

Female： Out most of villagers to play

从下游到上

From the downstream to top

那位像情哥

Who is my favorite brother

站木棉树下

Under kapok tree he stands great

男： 哪个在那边

Male： Who is the girl over there

像瓜花开放

As fresh as pumpkin flower[6]

像马蜂飞翔

Like a wasp[7] spreads its wings

似春燕轻盈

Walking on tiptoes coming near

女： 哪个在这里

Female： Who is the one near here

好似朵牡丹

So gorgeous like a peony

谁站在那里
Who is standing over there

像新结的瓜
Fresh as a new melon[8]

男： 踯躅在那里
Male： Over there she hesitantly standing

想飞又不去
Indecisive of leaving or staying

想飞翅不展
For its wings unwillingly vibrate

想走又想回
With frequent backward glimpse sheding

女： 踯躅在那里
Female： Over there he hesitantly standing

想飞又不去
Indecisive of leaving or staying

去了又转回
Pacing back and forth

这人是哪村
Which village is he from

男： 在那里踯躅
Male： She hesitantly standing over there

踯躅在那里

Over there she hesitantly standing

转似簸筛米

Turning around like sifting rice

或是惦记我[9]

Do I appear on your mind?

女： 在那里踯躅

Female： He hesitantly standing over there

踯躅在那里

Over there she[10] hesitantly standing[11]

嫩似棵姜苗

Tender as a ginger seedling

想撩他唱歌

Trying to ask him to sing

男： 在那眯眯笑

Male： So lovely you smile，as if

像彩蝶恋花

Over flower butterfly spreads wings

两眼轻轻眨

Frequently you stare at me

真是够风流

No one romantic than thy

女： 在那眯眯笑
Female： So joyously you smile，as if

像彩蝶恋花
Over flower butterfly spreads wings

嘴说眼凝视
Together，words and glances go

十分有诚意
With the affections I can see

男： 见花就想摘
Male： Seeing flowers my heart flies

见木叶想吹
Seeing leaves my music plays

与靓女相逢
The girl by chance meeting first

肯否对佯歌
Singing songs we both like?

女： 风和云相逢
Female： Of clouds the wind is soft

龙到此玩水
On water the dragon paddles

咱最喜欢玩
Having fun we both like

咱喜欢对歌
Antiphonal songs we like more

男： 与靓女相逢
Male： By chance we first meet

麒麟逢狮子
As the lion meets kylin[12]

与靓女相见
By chance we first meet

恩缘两相结
Together is the luck predestined

女： 与俊男相逢
Female： By chance we first meet

像蛟龙戏水
dragon paddling water alike

与俊男相见
By chance we first meet

恩缘结一起
Together is the luck predestined

男： 喜恩缘连结
Male： Grateful，connection between you and me

恩缘结一起
Together is the luck predestined

一起进枫林

Hand in hand into maple forest

咱同声唱歌

Sing songs of lunar March we need[13]

女: 喜恩缘连结

Female: Grateful，connection between you and me

恩缘结一起

Together is the luck predestined

一起进枫林

Hand in hand into maple forest

放声三月歌

Sing songs of lunar March we like

男: 喜恩缘相结

Male: Grateful，connection between you and me

铁锤砸石块

The hammer struck the stone

拿它来铺路

Laying stones to pave the road

好来往对歌

Connection for singing duet songs

女: 喜恩缘相结

Female: Grateful，connection between you and me

铁锤砸石块

The hammer struck the stone

拿它来铺路

Using stones to pave the road

通往三月歌

Sing songs of lunar March we love

男： 头歌到此止

Male： So much for the opening song

咱另起新声

Let's make a new voice

咱另唱新调

Let's make a new start

咱唱三月歌

And sing lunar March songs heartly

女： 头歌到此止

Female： So much for the opening song

咱另起新声

Let's make a new voice

哥你会歌多

Brother you sing more songs

你先开个头

You'd better take a lead

唱花 Singing Flowers

男：   菩叶似碗口
Male： Pomelo[14] leaves big as bowl

再不找冬衣
Winter clothes have yet done[15]

木棉树叶遮鸦翅
Kapok trees hide a crow

冬去不复回
Winter goes and never comes

女：   菩叶似碗口
Female： Pomelo leaves big as bowl

再不找冬衣
Winter clothes have yet done

木棉树叶遮鸦翅
Kapok trees hide a crow

冬去不复回
Winter goes and never comes

男：　　二三月天晴
Male：　In lunar February and March it is fine

人人脱棉衣
Winter clothes we put aside

收棉衣进笼
Winter clothes put in closet

同唱三月歌
Lunar March songs sing as we like

女：　　二三月惊蛰
Female：Lunar February and March awaken insects

人人脱棉衣
Winter clothes we put aside

收棉衣进笼
Winter clothes put in closet

同唱三月歌
Lunar March songs sung as we like

男：　　古时真会造
Male：　In old times people created

老辈真会制
Old stuff all hand-made

制笠又制伞
Hats and umbrellas they had made

想唱三月歌
Lunar March songs together we play

女： 古时真会造
Female： In old times people created
老辈真会制
Old stuff all hand-made

制斗笠蓑衣
Hats and coir raincoat they had made

想唱三月歌
Lunar March songs together we play

男： 二三月风大
Male： In lunar February and March it is windy

落叶满山谷
Maple leaves cover the valley

山谷叶堆满
Among piles of fallen leaves

满山黑衣娟
Crowds of girls are in black

女： 二三月风大
Female： In lunar February and March it is windy

落叶满山谷
Maple leaves cover the valley

山谷叶相混

Various leaves all mixed up

满山白衣冒
Crowds of boys are in white

男：　二三月风多
Male：　In lunar February and March it is windy

竹叶落街巷
Bamboo leaves fall on alley

一半已成娘
Half of girls become mothers

一半来对歌
Singing songs are the others

女：　二三月风多
Female：In lunar February and March it is windy

竹叶落街巷
Bamboo leaves fall on alley

一半已成爹
Half of boys become fathers

也跑来对唱
Singing songs are the others

男：　二三月风刮
Male：　In lunar February and March it is windy

催树枝发芽

Breeze blows trees in bud

芽发百种树
Buds grow into hundreds of trees

哪种树先发
Which sprout earlier do you know?

女： 二三月风刮
Female：In lunar February and March it is windy

催树枝发芽
Breeze blows trees in bud

芽发百种树
Buds grow into hundreds of trees

松树它先发
Pine tree sprouts the earliest

男： 腊月树抽芽
Male： Trees sprout in winter month

正月树含苞
In lunar January trees are in bud

百树长新叶
New leaves on trees grow

哪种树先长
Which is first we all know

女： 腊月树抽芽

Female：Trees sprout in winter month

正月树含苞
In lunar January trees are in bud

百树长新叶
New leaves on trees grow

枫树最先长
Maple the first we all know

男： 二三月含蕾
Male： Lunar Febraury and March buds more

不意花先开
Unexpectly all is in blossom

菰花开屋旁
Gux[16] blooming around my house

萠花蔓柔嫩
Baemh[17] growing tender and gorgeous

女： 二三月含蕾
Female： Lunar Febraury and March buds more

不意花先开
Unexpectly all is in blossom

菰花开屋旁
Gux blooming around my house

萠花蔓柔嫩

Baemh growing tender and gorgeous

男： 百树长新芽
Male： Darling buds all in trees

千树发新枝
Trees turn green in their leaves

满山披新绿
Fresh green covers all mountains

哪一山最先
Which the first turn green?

女： 百树长新芽
Female： Darling buds all in trees

千树发新枝
Trees turn green in their leaves

满山披新绿
Fresh green covers all mountains

楠树它最先
Raq[18] the first to turn green

男： 二三月花开
Male： In lunar Febraury and March flowers are in bloom

催人出来玩
Attract folks out to enjoy

玩过一坡坡

Walking on many a mount

哪山合对歌
Singing songs in which mount?

女： 二三月花开
Female： In lunar Febraury and March flowers are in bloom

催众人来玩
Attract folks out to enjoy

玩过一坡坡
Walking on many a mount

莫圩合对歌
Sing Songs in Haw Mo(z)[19]

男： 二三月花开
Male： In lunar Febraury and March flowers are in bloom

夹在树丫里
Between trunks and forks all

挂在树枝上
Hanging on the branches still

哪村合唱歌
Where sing songs to go for?

女： 二三月枉花
Female： In lunar February and March va vengj[20] are in bloom

开放在枝头

Branches they are hanging on

开枝头不谢
Never fade or fall

莫圩合对歌
Sing Songs in Haw Mo(z)

男： 二三月花开
Male： In lunar Febraury and March flowers are in bloom

催人出来玩
Attract folks out to enjoy

游玩到街上
Walking on many streets

见黄花中意
Va mai[21] flowers please me

女： 二三月花开
Female： In lunar Febraury and March flowers are in bloom

催人出来玩
Attract folks out to enjoy

游玩到街上
Walking on many streets

见黄花开心
Va mai flowers delight me

男： 二三月花开

Male： In lunar Febraury and March flowers are in bloom

催人出来玩
Attract folks out to enjoy

来到蔗园地
Come and play in the Han's[22]

见枉花中意
Va vengj flowers please me

女： 二三月花开
Female： In lunar Febraury and March flowers are in bloom

催人出来玩
Attract folks out to enjoy

来到蔗园地
Come and play in the Han's

见枉花开心
Va vengj flowers delight me

男： 二三月花开
Male： In lunar Febraury and March flowers are in bloom

催人出来玩
Attract folks out to enjoy

游玩到河边
On the river bank we play

见桃花中意

Delight me peach blossoms made

女： 二三月花开
Female： In lunar Febraury and March flowers are in bloom

催人出来玩
Attract folks out to enjoy

游玩到河边
On the river bank we play

见桃花开心
Delight me peach blossoms made

男： 李花白连连
Male： Bright white plum blossoms like

桃花红艳艳
Bright red peach blossoms like

艳不过桃花
None's so glamorous as peach blossoms

白不过情妹
None's as my lover so white

女： 李花白连连
Female： Bright white plum blossoms like

桃花红艳艳
Bright red peach blossoms like

艳不过桃花

None's so glamorous as peach blossoms

白不过情哥
None's as my lover so white

男： 李花正盛开
Male： Clusters of plum blossoms in sight

苓花正怒放
Clusters of limh bloom wide

情妹正含苞
My love girl is in bud

真引人羡慕
How charming is my lover

女： 李花正盛开
Female： Clusters of plum blossoms in sight

苓花正怒放
Clusters of limh bloom wide

情哥正含苞
My love boy is in bud

真令人喜爱
How handsome is my lover

男： 断久不进山
Male： Haven't been to mountains for long

不想花已盛

Unexpectly flowers in high bloom

要知花盛开
Wanna know flower blooming

咱早过来玩
Come earlier and we play

女： 断久不进山
Female： Haven't been to mountains for long

不想花已盛
Unexpectly flowers in high bloom

人早争去恋
A mountain of young girls[23]

咱后面才去
I would be the last to come

男： 我俩到此玩
Male： We come here to find

见两塘荷花
Lotus in two ponds stay

荷花轻摇头
Shaking slightly its head

扰咱心头乱
It has disturbed my mind

女： 我俩到此玩

Female：We come here to find

见两塘荷花
Lotus in two ponds stay

荷花轻摇头
Shaking slightly its head

风来点头拜
It nods as the breeze blows

男：　　过这塘边来
Male：　We come at the pond

见荷花聚拢
Cluster of lotus in sight

花边拢边开
In blossom or in bud

魂断在塘边
Being in an ecstasy of delight

女：　　过这塘边来
Female：We come at the pond

见荷花盛开
Cluster of lotus in sight

朵比朵鲜美
One's fresher than another

陶醉了情哥

My lover he is delighted

男： 南瓜花在那
Male： Pumpkin's in blossom over there

水瓜花在这
Towel gourd's in blossom near here

妹姣美艳丽
You are nice and bright

福气大过人
With better fortune than others

女： 南瓜花在那
Female： Pumpkin's in blossom over there

水瓜花在这
Towel gourd's in blossom near here

哥伟岸脱俗
You are handsome and smart

福气不属咱[24]
Bless me not but others'

男： 在远看麦花
Male： Buckwheat flowers are in distance

白花花像银
White as silver in the field

在远见观音

I see my lover in distance

能近不能叫
Try in vain to talk to her

女： 在远看麦花
Female：Buckwheat flowers are in distance

田垌白茫茫
White as silver in the field

在远见情郎
I see my lover in distance

行路步踉跄
I stumble on my way

男： 三月花盛开
Male： In lunar March flowers are in full bloom

菰花开桥下
Gux blooming under bridge

桥下人很多
Many people standing there

可惜不能掐
Pity that flower is beyond me

女： 三月花盛开
Female： In lunar March flowers are in full bloom

菰花开桥下

Gux blooming under bridge

桥下人很多
Many people standing there

死也扣不着
Pity that I can't reach for it

男：　桃花开满坡
Male：　A mountain of peach blossoms

不如朵牡丹
None's so bright as a peony

姑娘一帮帮
Clouds of young girls there

不如妹可爱
None's so pretty as my lover

女：　桃花开满坡
Female：A mountain of peach blossoms

不如朵红棉
None's so bright as a kapok

满山的青年
Clouds of young boys there

哥伟岸过人
None's so handsome as my lover

男：　花开香遍地

Male： Blossoms fragrant here and there

不如玉兰香
None's as sweet as a magnolia

姑娘上万千
Clouds of young girls there

不比情妹甜
None's so sweet as my lover

女： 花开香遍地
Female： Blossom fragrant here and there

不比茉莉香
None's as sweet as jasmine

多少人漂亮[25]
So many people all aroud the world

靓不比情哥
None's so handsome as my lover

男： 花开多姣艳
Male： Flowers are fresh and bright

像新棉刚弹
Soft as newly fluffed cotton

似蘸毛雏鹅
Pretty as newly born goose

想摸它逃脱

Wanna touch her but she escapes

女： 花开多姣艳
Female：Flowers are fresh and bright

像新棉刚弹
Soft as newly fluffed cotton

想和他攀友
Wanna make him my friend

怕友嫌咱老
But fear my age he'd mind

男： 花满山
Male： A mountain of flowers there

开山顶树梢
In bloom on the tree

手摘摘不到
Can't reach them by hand

竿打打不着
Nor touch her with a bamboo pole

女： 花满山
Female：A mountain of flowers there

开山顶树梢
In bloom on the tree

花开不姣艳

Who cares flowers bright or not

自开自凋落
Bloom on their own and fade

男： 这园花鲜艳
Male： Flowers nice and bright

有朵出园边
One's out of the garden

我想去赏玩
Longing for enjoying it

埂高难攀上
The ridge is too high to climb

女： 这园花鲜艳
Female： Flowers nice and bright

有朵出藩篱
One's out of the fence

想挣脱出去
Longing for breaking free

恨荆篱阻隔
But the fence's too high

男： 花盛开
Male： Flowers are full in blossom

开在别人园

Bloom in others' garden

人看眼不眨
Being seen without a blink

只得空窥探
Distance it is in my sight

女： 花盛开
Female： Flowers are full in blossom

开在哥园中
Bloom in my lover's[26] garden

果红等哥掐
Fruits ripen for you to pick

花红等哥赏
Flowers fresh for you to enjoy

男： 我想去赏花
Male： Long for enjoy the flower

恨条河阻挡
A grand river on the way

恨座山阻隔
A high mountain on the way

我只得空归
Try to reach but in vain

女： 不怕条河阻

Female：Fear not the grand river

不怕座山隔
Fear not the high mountain

倒怕你情哥
Only fear that my lover

不伸手去摘
Not reach out for the flower

男：　花开在水边
Male：　Flowers on the river bank

恨这水阻隔
Kept away by the river

我得问情妹
Sincerely I ask my dear

肯不肯伸手
Long for connecting me or not

女：　花开在河边
Female：Flowers on the river bank

想过没有桥
Can't cross without a bridge

两边心相照
As love felt for each other

水自退自消

Water'd run dry and disappear

男： 花对花
Male： Flower to flower

花开在两岸
Bloom on the river banks

几时水变石
Whenever stones come out of water

咱易爬过去
Easily cross the river I can

女： 花对花
Female： Flower to flower

花开在两岸
Bloom on the river banks

今日水变石
Today stones come out of water

怕你也不过
Worry if you cross over

男： 花四季
Male： Four seasons are flowers bright

得意开天上
In high bloom we like

咱想上去赏

We'd enjoy in the sky

找不到途径
But no path we can find

女： 花四季
Female：Four seasons are flowers bright

得意开天上
In high bloom we like

你想要啊哥
If you long for flowers

托群鸟去叫
Ask for help of birds

男： 花儿红
Male： Flowers red

开在刺丛中
Bloom deep in the thorns

想用竿去钩
Get them with a stick

怕荆棘刺手
Fear that thorns prick my hand

女： 花儿红
Female：Flowers red

开在刺丛中

Bloom deep in the thorns

想踮脚去钩
On tiptoe you pick flowers

把荆棘踏平
And trod down the thorns

男： 山花开
Male： Mountain flowers bloom

在悬崖藤上
High on the cliff vine

我想折想拉
I want to pick them

怕崖塌惊天
Fear that the cliff'd fall

女： 山花开
Female： Mountain flowers bloom

在悬崖藤上
High on the cliff vine

你想折想拉
You want to pick them

崖塌花跟去
Flowers go with falling cliff

男： 花彤红

Male： The flower is lovely red

同真想去拔
How I long for picking it

连根一起拔
By the roots I'd pull out

围园拿来栽
Round the garden and I plant

女： 花彤红
Female： The flower is lovely red

同慢过去拔
Wanna slowly pick it[27]

有心拔回去
Pull it back if you intend to

栽石上也活
Even on stone it can grow

男： 花可爱
Male： The flower is lovely red

十分想去摸
Attracting me to caress it

摸又怕它凋
But fear it would fade

包又怕它谢

Or wither if in packet

女： 花可爱
Female： The flower is lovely red

哥有心去摘
Please pick it if long for

花开等飞燕
For swallow it is waiting

花艳等情哥
For my lover it is blooming

男： 花盛开
Male： Flowers nice and bright

开满山满坡
Bloom all over the mountain

若没有蜂过
Without bee coming for honey

花谢难结果
The flower'd fade without fruits

女： 花盛开
Female： Flowers are nice and bright

开满山满坡
Bloom all over the mountain

天天有蜂过

The bee comes for honey daily

但仍在等哥
The flower for you still waits

男： 花开天过天
Male： Flowers are bright day by day

花红季算季
Flowers red year after year

明日花老了
Tomorrow the flower'd fade

当篱上干菜
As dried vegetable on the fence

女： 花开天过天
Female： Flowers are bright day by day

花红季算季
Flowers are red year after year

明日老了哥
Tomorrow my lover gets older

心想事难成
Spirits stay but the flesh weak

男： 花开不引蝶
Male： Flowers not attract butterflies

花算是白开

All the efforts are in vain

长大不去恋
Young girls not to love

枉费好年华
Good times you'd waste

女： 花开不出色
Female： Flowers are not nice and bright

似桌上菜花[28]
As dried potherbs on the table

花四开四谢
Flowers bloom and fade

蝶爱就来栖
Butterflies are attracted to enjoy

插花 Wearing Flowers

男： 桃花正盛开
Male： Peach flower is full in bloom

人人争去采
Everybody rush to pick it

咱也采来插
And I pick and wear it

不插花就谢
Or it would fade very soon

女： 桃花正盛开
Female： Peach flower is full in bloom

人人争去采
To pick it everybody rush

咱也采来插
And I pick and wear it

眨眼花就枯
It would fade very soon

男： 此时不插花

Male： Flower not worn today

花一朝一夕

It would fade in one day

明日老才插

Worn tomorrow it would fade

你崽就拔出

Kids'd pull it out and throw it away

女： 此时不插花

Female： Flowers not worn today

花一朝一夕

It would fade in one day

明日老才插

Worn tomorrow it would fade

花十色九样

They would be fresh no way

男： 将来老了妹

Male： We would be old one day

插花也不美

Not so pretty with flower

不美似当年

Not beautiful as the old days'

不艳似情妹
Nor as dear as my lover

女： 将来老了同
Female：We would be old one day

插红花不美
Not so smart with flower

不美似当年
Not so handsome as the old days'

不艳似十八
Nor as dear as my lover

男： 此时不插花
Male： Flowers not worn today

树上花就落
Would wither and fade away

花就落到根
Flowers fall to the root

真的落到地
And they'd fall to the ground

女： 此时不插花
Female：Flowers not worn today

树上花就落
Would wither and fade away

花就落到地
Flowers fall to the ground

落地还再生
And revival in the wood

男： 插花别插密
Male： Do not wear flowers too many

到发际即可
A few on the hair is nice[29]

去恋莫去早
Do not fall in love too early

会错过好人
Or someone you'll miss

女： 插花别插密
Female： Do not wear flowers too many

发际插两朵
Two on the hair is nice

去恋可要早
Do love your girl early

晚就空手回
Or you'll return with hands empty

男： 插花别插密
Male： Do not wear flowers too many

到鬓际即可

A few at the temples is nice

去恋别多去

Do not love too many

多去会死人

Or somebody for you would die

女： 插花别插密

Female： Do not wear flowers too many

到鬓际即可

A few on the hair is nice

去恋别多去

Do not love too many

学会即回来

Return when your love's found

男： 插花同插花

Male： Both of us wear flowers

花相缠相拖

Which are put in disorder

插花不利索

So clumsy-handed we are

人见多取笑

The others would laugh at us

女：　　插花同插花
Female：Both of us wear flowers

　　　　花相拖相叠
　　　　Which are put in disorder

　　　　插花易相随
　　　　Flowers mixed up in a mess

　　　　插红花映面
　　　　Shining upon your face red

男：　　插花同插花
Male：　Both of us wear flowers

　　　　花相缠相拖
　　　　In disorder they are put

　　　　不多插一朵
　　　　Wear not more than others

　　　　别人就会说
　　　　Or we'd be laughed at

女：　　插花同插花
Female：Both of us wear flowers

　　　　花相缠相拖
　　　　In disorder they are put

　　　　插不过别人
　　　　Less skillful than the others

我俩真不信
But we'd never loss our hearts

男： 插花同插花
Male： Both of us wear flowers

不要插茶花
Do not wear camellia flowers

果还未熟花又开
It blooms again before fruits grow

转脸又再找别人
As your lover turns away for others

女： 插花同插花
Female： Both of us wear flowers

不要插茶花
Do not wear camellia flowers

果还未熟花又开
It blooms again before its seeds have ripened

花开果就落
Fruits fall when flowers bloom

男： 插花同插花
Male： Both of us wear flowers

插朵五彩花
Five-color flowers we wear

插不快人欺

The slower would be laughed at

插不好人侮

The unskillful would be teased

女： 插花同插花

Female： Both of us wear flowers

插朵五彩花

Five-color flowers we wear

插不好人笑

The clumsy would be laughed at

插不好人侮

The unskillful would be teased

男： 插花同插花

Male： Both of us wear flowers

插花占地府

It takes space to plant flowers[30]

去恋胜别人

My lover's better than old flame[31]

我俩才舒心

The more delighted we would be

女： 插花同插花

Female： Both of us wear flowers

插花占地府

The better one we long to wear

去恋胜别人

My lover's better than the others

我俩才舒服

The more delighted we would be

男： 插花同插花

Male： Both of us wear flowers

插两丛插筒[32]

With two bunches in the pot

明日出去插

We'd out tomorrow for flowers

花十色九样

They would be fresh no way

女： 插花同插花

Female： Both of us wear flowers

插两丛插筒

With two bunches in the pot

明日出去插

We'd out tomorrow for flowers

花鲜艳皎洁

White, fresh and bright

男： 不插花就完

Male： Flowers'd fade if no one wears them

不采花就谢

They would fade away if no one picks them

凋谢在枝头

Flowers wither on the branch

飘浮落在地

And perish on the ground forever

女： 不插花就完

Female： Flowers'd fade if no one wears them

不采花就谢

They would fade away if no one picks them

凋谢在枝头

Flowers wither on the branch

飘浮落在地

And perish on the ground forever

男： 桐花朵朵鲜

Male： Tung flowers fresh and bright

十有九会谢

Nine out of ten would fade

哥问你情妹

I'd like to ask my sweetheart

哪朵开不败
Which one would bloom forever?

女： 桐花朵朵鲜
Female： Tung³³ flowers fresh and bright

朵朵都会谢
One day they all would fade

妹告诉情哥
I'd like to tell my sweetheart

没有常年花
No flower could bloom all day

男： 今日遇新花
Male： A new flower I meet today

不知名就查
Her name I don't know

妹你告诉我
Tell me your name my sweetheart

让我挖去栽
Let me bring it home to plant

女： 今日遇新花
Female： A new flower I meet today

你不知就查
Check it if you don't know her name

告诉你实话
Tell you the truth my sweetheart

寡花不结果
A single flower bears no fruit

男： 今天遇红花
Male： A red flower I meet today

不知名就问
Then I ask her name

等我挖回家
I'd like to bring it home

栽楼外观赏
Plant it outdoors for enjoyment

女： 今天遇红花
Female： A red flower I meet today

不知名就问
Then I ask his name

告诉你了哥
Tell you the truth my sweetheat

有心栽才开
Only a love flower would bloom

男： 见花开对岸
Male： Flower on the other bank

下河过去采

Going across the river for it

身沉河中央

Into the river I'd sink

为花亡心甘

I would die for my flower

女： 那花是瓜花

Female： Pumpkin flower blooms

日晒它就萎

In the hot sun it'd wither

说给你了哥

Tell you the truth my sweetheart

为何为花死

Why would die for the flower?

男： 艳花开桥边

Male： Flowers bloom by the bridge

鲜花浮河面

All floating on the river

有船的人能观赏

With boats they could enjoy them

咱没有船空遗憾

Pity is that I have no boat

女： 艳花开桥边
Female： Flowers bloom by the bridge

鲜花浮河面
All floating on the river

无船去观赏
I could not go without boat

看花流下滩
Seeing flowers floating away

男： 我俩折要花
Male： We reach out for the flower

花落水下滩
Flower falls into the river

我命是寡命
Being out of luck

赏花空手回
I return home with empty hands

女： 想要花吗哥
Female： Do you long for a flower?

花落有花开
Flowers bloom and wither

摘朵给你戴
Pick one for you to wear

男人戴不惯

As men refuse to wear them

男： 妹在塘边站

Male： By the pond she is standing

咱叫妹赏花

I ask her to enjoy the flower

她转脸不看

There she is away turning

花谢完凋尽

And the flower falls and fade

女： 哥在塘边站

Female： By the pond he is standing

咱叫哥赏花

I ask him to enjoy the flower

他转脸来看

There he turns and enjoys it

花开完开尽

And the flower is in full blossom

叹蝉 Singing Cicada

男： 百花已开尽
Male： Hundreds of flowers after high blossom

木棉花未开
Except the red kapok flower

连瓢花瓜花
Gourds and melons start to bloom

年年开四月
They all bloom every lunar April

女： 百花已开尽
Female： Hundreds of flowers after high blossom

木棉还未开
Except the red kapok flower

清明开木棉
Kapok starts to bloom in Qingming

花全开了哥
And all plants are in blossom

男：　　百花已开尽
Male：　Hundreds of flowers after high blossom

　　　　木棉正含苞
　　　　Red kapok still in bud

　　　　过二月三月
　　　　From lunar February and March on

　　　　到哪能遇妹
　　　　Where my lover I can meet?

女：　　样样花开尽
Female：Hundreds of flowers after high blossom

　　　　木棉花就开
　　　　Red kapok still in blossom

　　　　到了二三月
　　　　From lunar February and March on

　　　　去哪对山歌
　　　　Where to sing songs with you?

男：　　李花正盛开
Male：　Plum is in full blossom

　　　　苓花才结蕾
　　　　And limz[34] is still budding

　　　　二月它才开
　　　　It starts to bloom in lunar February

花开到三月

And to lunar March it would last

女： 木棉花盛开

Female： Kapok is in full blossom

捻花才结蕾

Myrtle is still budding

四月它才开

To bloom in lunar April it starts

花开到五月

And to lunar May it would last

男： 天初暖

Male： Warm it is getting day by day

鱼转头向泉

Head to the spring fish turn

走路有风吹

Wind blows as one is walking

靓女有人占

Pretty folk girls long to own

女： 天初暖

Female： Warm it is getting day by day

鱼转头向泉

Head to the spring fish turn

走路有人跟

Followed by others as one is walking

俊男有人占

Smart folk boys long to own

男：　二三月多雨

Male： Many rainfalls in lunar February and March

今日雨转阴

Today rain turns to overcast

与知心同行

With my lover I'd like to go

与情妹对歌

With my sweetheart I'd sing

女：　二三月多雨

Female： Many rainfalls in lunar February and March

今日雨转阴

Today rain turns to overcast

爱与哥游戏

With my lover I'd like to play

爱与哥对歌

With my sweetheart I'd sing

男：　二三月转暖

Male： Warmer it is in lunar February and March

鱼向泉调头

Head to the spring fish turn

走路有风推

Wind pushing as one is walking

好妹有人订

Pretty girl folks long to own

女： 二三月转暖
Female： Warmer it is in lunar February and March

鱼向泉调头

Head to the spring fish turn

走路有风推

Wind pushing as one is walking

美哥有人赞

Smart boy folks long to extol

男： 二三月转暖
Male： Warmer it is in lunar February and March

鱼转头向河

Head to the river fish turn

河边花正红

Flowers red by the river

旧友人已占

Old friend folks have owned

女：　二三月转暖

Female： Warmer it is in lunar February and March

鱼转头向河

Head to the river fish turn

哪个已占我

Who longs to own me?

哪个愿娶奴

Who longs to marry me?

男：　二三月转暖

Male： Warmer it is in lunar February and March

穿布衣嫌痒

Cotton cloths rough and hot

穿六合嫌粗

Patched cloths heavy and coarse

穿啥才合意

Which cloths soft and comfortable?

女：　二三月转暖

Female： Warmer it is in lunar February and March

穿布衣嫌痒

Cotton cloths rough and hot

穿六合嫌粗

Patched cloths heavy and coarse

穿纱才合意

Gauze cloths best fit

男： 二三月转暖

Male： Warmer it is in lunar February and March

穿布衣嫌痒

Cotton cloths rough and hot

穿六合嫌刺

Patched cloths heavy and coarse

头枕臂出汗

One sweats lying on bed

女： 二三月转暖

Female： Warmer it is in lunar February and March

穿布衣嫌痒

Cotton cloths rough and hot

穿六合嫌刺

Patched cloths heavy and coarse

头枕臂臭汗

Smelly sweat pillowed on my arm

男： 二三月转暖

Male： Warmer it is in lunar February and March

妹跳栏又打陀螺

Playing jump games with joys

妹打陀螺在街上

Beating spinning top in the streets

饭不吃也饱

Feeling full without eating meals

女： 二三月转暖

Female：Warmer it is in lunar February and March

哥跳栏又打陀螺

Playing jump games with joys

哥打陀螺在街上

Beating spinning top in the streets

饭要父亲送

Dinner your dad had to send

男： 二三月转暖

Male： Warmer it is in lunar February and March

妹跳栏又打陀螺

Playing jump games with joys

妹打陀螺在城外

Beating spinning top outside the city

饭不吃也饱

Feeling full without eating meals

女： 二三月转暖

Female：Warmer it is in lunar February and March

哥跳栏又打陀螺

Playing jump games with joys

哥打陀螺在城外

Beating spinning top outside the city

饭要父亲送

Dinner your dad had to send

男：　二三月转暖

Male： Warmer it is in lunar February and March

妹跳栏又打陀螺

Playing jump games with joys

妹打陀螺在楼下

Beating spinning top downstairs

饭不吃也饱

Feeling full without eating meals

女：　二三月转暖

Female： Warmer it is in lunar February and March

哥跳栏又打陀螺

Playing jump games with joys

哥打陀螺在楼下

Beating spinning top downstairs

饭要父亲送

Dinner your dad had to send

男： 二三月转暖
Male： Warmer it is in lunar February and March

妹去桥利打陀螺
Beating spinning top in Qiaoli

四十天不见回来
She hasn't be back for 40 days

咱卖田去赎
I'd sell land for her redeem

女： 二三月转暖
Female： Warmer it is in lunar February and March

哥去桥利打陀螺
Beating spinning top in Qiaoli

四十天不见回来
He hasn't be back for 40 days

咱卖布去赎
I'd sell cloth for his redeem

男： 二三月转暖
Male： Warmer it is in lunar February and March

我到这里玩
Having fun I come here

今天好运气
A good day it is today

得与妹相遇
Meeting my lover here today

女： 二三月转暖
Female： Warmer it is in lunar February and March

我到这里玩
Having fun I come here

今天好运气
A good day it is today

得与妹相逢
Meeting my lover here today

男： 天晴朗
Male： It is sunny it is fine

山雀衔蜻蜓
With dragonfly in the mouth

衔蜻蜓进园
Skylark flies into the garden

哪月能见妹
Which month I could see my lover?

女： 天晴朗
Female： It is sunny it is fine

山雀衔蜻蜓
With dragonfly in the mouth

衔蜻蜓进园
Skylark flies into the garden

正月刚见你
I just met you this lunar January

男: 天晴朗
Male: It is sunny it is fine

蜂荫处造巢
Beehive's built in the shade

同片田片地
The same field over there

就不遇情妹
But my lover I couldn't meet

女: 天晴朗
Female: It is sunny it is fine

蜂荫处造巢
Beehive's built in the shade

同片地片田
The same field over there

不见哥外出
But my lover's not going out

男: 天晴朗
Male: It is sunny it is fine

蜂伞下造巢

Under the umbrella is nesting bee

夫妻培小米

Cultivating millet you couple together

哪里想到我

No time for me you'd spare

女： 天晴朗

Female：It is sunny it is fine

蜂伞下造巢

Under the umbrella is nesting bee

你妻多美貌

So beautiful is your wife

哪会想到我

No time for me you'd spare

男： 天晴朗

Male：It is sunny it is fine

钱菜死地边

Centella withers on the field

莳菜死深潭

Wild herbs in the deep pond die

找菜人晕懵

The potherb-seekers dizzy head

女：　　天晴朗
Female：It is sunny it is fine

钱菜死地边
Centella withers on the field

蔊菜死烂田
Wild herbs in the muddy field die

情妹死田垌
She's left dead in the field

男：　　天晴朗
Male：　It is sunny it is fine

蝉四处鸣叫
Cicada singing songs wherever it flies

鸣叫声连声
Its chirping's on and on

令我心头乱
Making my fancy away fly

女：　　天晴朗
Female：It is sunny it is fine

到时蝉就鸣
Cicada singing songs in time

鸣上又鸣下
It's heard up and down

个个找情人

For his own love one is to find

男： 三百六只蝉

Male： 360 cicadas together over there

哪只蝉先叫

Which one singing first

先鸣叫吱吱

The call of cicadas sounds better

妹你告诉我

Please tell me my sweetheart

女： 三百六只蝉

Female： 360 cicadas together over there

枫树蝉先叫

On maple trees it sings first

先鸣叫吱吱

The call of cicadas sounds better

告知你就记

Please keep it in your mind

男： 我问你只蝉

Male： Let me ask you the cicada

冷时到哪躲

Where to shelter from the cold?

饿时到哪吃

Where to find food when hungry?

春时出来叫

Then chirping in spring it starts

女：　我说这只蝉

Female： Let me tell you the cicada

冷时它冬眠

It hibernates when it's cold

冬眠到清明

In Qingming it comes out

才放声鸣叫

Singing out loud it starts

男：　蝉吱吱鸣叫

Male： Cicadas singing songs over there

鸣叫枫树荫

Chirping on the shadow of maple trees

蝉声清又脆

Clear and crisp cicadas sound

催妹去婆家

Urge you to go to your husband's

女：　蝉吱吱鸣叫

Female： Cicadas singing songs over there

鸣叫枫树荫

Chirping on the shadow of maple trees

蝉声清又脆

Clear and crisp cicadas sound

催你妻回来

Urge your wife to come home

男： 蝉吱吱鸣唱

Male： Cicadas singing songs over there

庭前枫树上

On the maples in the yard

催枉树[35]抽芽

Urge golden blossom to have bud

催妹去婆家

Urge you to go to your husband's

女： 蝉吱吱鸣唱

Female： Cicadas singing songs over there

庭前枫树上

On the maples in the yard

催枉树抽芽

Urge trees to have bud

催你妻回家

Urge your wife to go home

男： 蝉吱吱鸣唱

Male： Cicadas singing songs over there

泉边椀树上

At the spring on Cherokee rose

蝉山泉旁叫

By the fountain they sing

叫你回婆家

Urge you to go back to your husband's

女： 蝉吱吱鸣唱

Female： Cicadas singing songs over there

泉边椀树上

At the spring on Cherokee rose

蝉天泉上叫

By the fountain they sing

叫你去田垌

Urge you to go to the field

男： 别再叫了蝉

Male： Do not chirp any more

冬天已将过

As winter is passing by

你将回婆家

You will go to your husband's

去了别忘我

Forget me not when you go

女： 别再叫了蝉

Female：Do not chirp any more

冬天已将过

As winter is passing by

咱没婆家去

Have not been to my husband's

时时在娘家

But to stay in my mom's

男： 别再叫了蝉

Male：Do not chirp any more

怕你翘膀伤

Lest you'd hurt your wings

别再叫了妹

Do not sing any more

怕你嗓音坏

Lest you'd hurt your voice

女： 别再叫了蝉

Female：Do not chirp any more

怕你翘膀伤

Lest you'd hurt your wings

别再叫了哥

Do not sing any more

怕你嗓音哑

Lest you'd hurt your voice

男: 别再叫了蝉
Male: Do not chirp any more

怕你翅膀疼

Lest you'd hurt your wings

别再叫了妹

Do not sing any more

怕你嗓音痛

Lest you'd hurt your voice

女: 蝉吱吱鸣唱
Female: Chirping delightedly are the cicadas

不怕翅膀疼

Never fear the wings'd hurt

蝉本有嗓音

Be born with voice of melodies

不怕嗓音痛

Never fear the voice'd hurt

男: 别再叫了蝉
Male: Do not chirp any more

怕你翅膀折

Lest you'd hurt your wings

别再叫了妹

Do not sing any more

怕你色彩褪

Lest your love'd fade away

女： 蝉吱吱鸣唱

Female： Chirping delightedly are the cicadas

不怕折翅膀

Never fear the wings'd hurt

咱唱情唱爱

Love songs we would sing

怕啥色彩褪

Never fear the voice'd hurt

男： 蝉昂首鸣叫

Male： Cicadas chirping with head high

一天叫到晚

Singing from dawn till dark

喊声高声低

Their voices low or high

日斜声才止

Never stop before dusk

女： 蝉昂首鸣叫

Female：Cicadas chirping with head high

一天叫到晚

Singing from dawn till dark

喊声高声低

Their voices low or high

日西斜才停

Never stop before dusk

男： 听蝉叫喊声

Male： The songs cicadas sing I hear

真不想做人

I would rather be a bird

听到妹声音

The sound of my lover I hear

想做人又不想做

I'd rather be a bird than a man[36]

女： 听蝉叫喊声

Female：The songs cicadas sing I hear

真不想做人

I would rather be a bird

听到你声音

The sound of my lover I hear

想做人真不容易
It's not easy being human

男： 听蝉叫声喧
Male： I hear cicadas chirping

两翅悠悠颤
With two wings trembling

听蝉叫声脆
Voice of cicadas clear

有泪哭不出
Feel like crying but yield no tears

女： 听蝉叫声脆
Female： I hear cicadas chirping

眼泪落嘀嗒
My tears keep falling down

听蝉叫声幽
Voice of cicadas clear

心头全粉碎
Makes me agitated and sad

男： 蝉在树上鸣
Male： Cicadas on the tree are chirping

咱坐石上泣
I'm on the stone crying

为人不聪明
Not smarter than the others

让情妹取笑
Laughed at by my lover

女： 蝉在树上鸣
Female： Cicadas on the tree are chirping

咱坐石上泣
I'm on the stone crying

为人不聪明
Not smarter than the others

似四月蝶飞
As upset as April butterflies

男： 蝉在树上叫
Male： Cicadas on the tree are chirping

我在树下哭
I'm under the tree crying

做人不出息
Being a good-for-nothing

让妹轻视我
Being despised by my lover

女： 蝉在树上叫
Female： Cicadas on the tree are chirping

我在树下哭
I'm under the tree crying

你夫妻恩爱
You loving spouse together

忘咱旧日情
Our love being despised by her

男：　蝉在树上叫
Male：Cicadas on the tree are chirping

我柁树下哭
I'm under dok[37] tree crying

我无家无业
No house, no money

让你蔑视我
Being despised by you

女：　蝉在树上叫
Female：Cicadas on the tree are chirping

我柁树下泣
I'm under dok tree crying

你有家有业
House and money behind you

哪敢蔑视你
Who dares to depise you?

男：　蝉在树上叫
Male：　Cicadas on the tree are chirping

　　我芒树下泣
　　I'm under mango tree crying

　　独自过日子
　　My life is lonely and dreary

　　妹哪里知道
　　Who ever cares about me?

女：　蝉在树上叫
Female：　Cicadas on the tree are chirping

　　你芒树下泣
　　Under mango tree you're crying

　　每天都有人送鞋
　　Someone sent you shoes everyday

　　为什么还总哭泣
　　Why are you crying all day?

男：　蝉在树上叫
Male：　Cicadas on the tree are chirping

　　我椋树下泣
　　Under myrtle tree I'm crying

　　没一个知心
　　Close friends I have none

哭声高声低

Crying sound loud or low

女：　蝉在树上叫

Female： Cicadas on the tree are chirping

你棯树下泣

Under myrtle tree you're crying

告诉你情哥

Tell you truth my lover

哭多心就碎

Heart is broken when tears dry

男：　为这蝉可惜

Male： Great pity for this cicada

为蜻蜓着急

Very worried about this dragonfly

为情妹叹气

Heavily sigh for my lover

为蝉鸣被骂

For cicada's chirping I'm blamed

女：　为这蝉可惜

Female： Great pity for this cicada

为蜻蜓着急

Very worried about this dragonfly

为情哥叹气
Heavily sigh for my lover

为情哥被骂
For my lover I'm blamed

情累 Feeling Tired

男： 二三月蝉累
Male： Cicadas tired in lunar February and March

六七月蜓累
Dragonflies tired in June and July

四五月牛累
Cattle tired in lunar April and May

人们全累垮
All folks tired and drawn

女： 二三月蝉累
Female： Cicadas tired in lunar February and March

六七月蜓累
Dragonflies tired in lunar June and July

四五月牛累
Cattle tired in lunar April and May

人们全累软
All folks tired and drawn

男: 天初热
Male: It is early hot day

哪个不觉累
Untired no one feels

纺纱人也晕
Spinning worker also dizzy

烧火人也喘
Light up fire also tiring

女: 天初热
Female: It is early hot day

哪个不觉累
Untired no one feels

纺纱人也喘
Spinning worker also gasping

捡菜人也倦
Potherb-picker also exhausted

男: 累为晴为雨
Male: Wearied for it's fine or rain

累为昙为阴
Wearied for it's sunny or cloudy

累为避闲言
Wearied for avoiding gossip

累为别人妻
Wearied for being the other's wife

女： 累为晴为雨
Female：Wearied for it's fine or rain

累为昙为阴
Wearied for it's sunny or cloudy

累为避闲言
Wearied for avoiding gossip

累为哥变心
Wearied for his heart changed

男： 越沉重越累
Male：Feeling heavier and wearier

累似牛套轭
Tired as a yoked cattle

累似贩盐客
Tired as a salt trade man

累似船无桨
Tired as a boat without a paddle

女： 越沉重越累
Female：Feeling heavier and wearier

累似牛套轭
Tired as a yoked cattle

累似贩盐客
Tired as a salt trade man

累似船十桨
Tired as the 10 paddles on boat

男： 越累越更累
Male： Feeling tired and tired

累似车不转
Tired as a unmoved waterwheel

累似没有妹
Tired as I have no lover

我比别人累
More tired than the others

女： 越累越更累
Female： Feeling tired and tired

累似车不转
Tired as a unmoved waterwheel

累似哥变心
Tired as his heart changed

累似情哥爱别人
Tired as he loved the others

男： 真够累
Male： Tired it is I could feel

累似车不转

Tired as a unmoved waterwheel

车不转风推

Wind pushes a unmoved wheel

没有妹就累

Feeling tired if without my lover

女： 真够累

Female： Tired it is I could feel

累似车不转

Tired as a unmoved waterwheel

车不转风推

Wind pushes a unmoved wheel

没恋情人论

Gossiped if without my lover

男： 真太累了妹

Male： Really tired I could feel

软似锅上糍

As sticky rice on the pot

软似火上锡

As soft as tin on fire

真累极累够

Really tired I could feel

女：　真太累了哥

Female：Really tired I could feel

软似锅上糍

As sticky rice on the pot

软似火上锡

As soft as tin on fire

真累极累够

Really tired I could feel

男：　真太累了妹

Male：Really tired I could feel

浮似鸭下滩

As lonely as a duck floating

歪似酒醉人

Staggered as getting drunk

累全聚我身

Tiredness on my body all over

女：　真太累了哥

Female：Really tired I could feel

浮似鹅下塘

As a goose floating on the pond

浮似水上萍

As lonely as duckweed floating

累极身倒地
I fall down out of tiredness

男： 想情妹太累
Male： Extremly tired missing my lover

想情妹将死
I'm dying when I miss her

父母叫不省
Unconscious when parents call me

闻妹声才醒
But awaken by her voice

女： 想情哥太累
Female： Extremly tired missing my lover

想情哥欲死
I'm dying when I miss him

牛踩脚不动
Unmoved when stamped by cattle

闻哥声才省
But awaken by his voice

男： 累得不得了
Male： Really tired I could feel

桐油炒菀菜
Tung oil fried with vanj leaves[38]

知妹不再提到我

My lover mentioned me no more

昨夜更倦怠

Wearier last night I could not sleep

女： 累得不得了

Female： Really tired I could feel

桐油炒菀菜

Tung oil fried with vanj leaves

情哥又再提到我

My lover mentioned me once more

昨夜更觉累

Wearier last night I could not sleep

男： 累得不得了

Male： Really tired I could feel

知妹做法事

A love spell she is casting I know

做法事就解

Untired when it is done

上坡才不累

Not tired even go up slope

女： 累得不得了

Female： Really tired I could feel

知哥打爱符
A love spell he is casting I know

打爱符才甜
Content when it is done

上山才不累
Not tired even climb mountain

男： 累得不得了
Male： Really tired I could feel

糯饭装两盒
Sticky rice is in two bowls

甜酒装两罐
Sweet wine is in two pots

有力唱歌了没有
Feeling energetic to sing song?

女： 累得不得了
Female： Really tired I could feel

糯饭装两盒
Sticky rice is in two bowls

甜酒装两罐
Sweet wine is in two pots

上山跑在前
Ahead running towards mountain

男： 累得不得了
Male： Really tired I could feel

芭蕉长林边
Bananas are by the wood

因累不能常来往
For hard work we couldn't meet

让妹另去跟别人
You leave for the other boy

女： 累得不得了
Female： Really tired I could feel

芭蕉长林边
Bananas are by the wood

因累不能常来往
For hard work we couldn't meet

让哥另娶了别人
Then you married the other girl

男： 累得不得了
Male： Really tired I could feel

芭蕉长岭脚
Bananas are by the hill

十分累了妹
Tired you are I could see

编筐让妹挑

Bamboo basket for you to carry

女： 累得不得了

Female：Really tired I could feel

芭蕉长岭脚

Bananas are by the hill

十分累了哥

Tired you are I could see

挑筐有少妇

Bamboo basket carried by your wife

男： 累得不得了

Male： Really tired I could feel

芭蕉长山脚

Bananas are by the hill

太累了情妹

Tired you are I could see

纱树[39]长地边

Gosa trees are by the field

女： 累得不得了

Female：Really tired I could feel

芭蕉长山脚

Bananas are by the hill

太累了情哥

Tired you are I could see

纱树遮阳光

Yarn trees shade the sun

男： 累得不得了

Male： Really tired I could feel

十分撬不动

Could hardly pry me out

十分动不了

Could hardly move me aside

十分累了妹

Exhausted you are I could see

女： 累得不得了

Female： Really tired I could feel

十分撬不动

Could hardly pry me out

十分动不了

Could hardly move me aside

十分累了哥

Exhausted you are I could see

男： 十分累了妹

Male： Exhausted you are I could see

身沉似患病
Feeling heavy like I'm sick

娘请巫到家
Mom invited a witch to home

求仙也无用
A pray to immortal is in vain

女： 十分累了哥
Female： Exhausted you are I could see

身沉似患病
Feeling heavy like I'm sick

叫娘去问仙
Ask Mom to pray for me

咱心里明白
A pray to ghost is in vain

找菜 Finding Vegetables

男： 今日什么日

Male： What day is it today?

转山不到头

Hilltop could not be reached

转不过山头

Nor mountain be over climbed

找不见情妹

Nor my sweetheart be found

女： 今日什么日

Female： What day is it today?

转山能到头

Hilltop could be reached

从上转到下

From up to down I look for

不见情哥面

My sweetheart could not be found

男： 今日什么日
Male： What day is it today?

从山转到峎
From rocky hills to flat land

从峎转到林
From flat land to jungle

通不到情妹
My sweetheart could not be found

女： 今日什么日
Female： What day is it today?

从山转到峎
From rocky hills to flat land

从峎转到林
From flat land to the woods

歌不通情哥
Songs I sing not accessible to you

男： 讲什么林里
Male： What to say in the woods?

知妹找苊菜
Mbonq leaves you're seeking

先去的得苗
Seedlings for the early comers

后去的得叶

While foliage for the late comers

女： 讲什么林里

Female：What to say in the woods?

知哥找耙齿

Harrow you are looking for

耙齿后天有

It is ready in two days

先坐下对歌

Together we sit and sing

男： 讲什么林里

Male： What to say in the woods?

知妹找苋菜

Mbonq[40] leaves you're seeking

苋菜未抽芽

Mbonq has not yet sprouted

丢裙先对歌

Put it aside for singing songs

女： 讲什么林里

Female：What to say in the woods?

知哥找耙齿

Harrow you are looking for

哪条合才砍
Right branch's good for harrow

哪条顶才要
Strong branch would be fine

男：　莳菜已抽芽
Male：　Already in bud is Mbonq

莳菜已长高
Tall enough it grows

妹你就去要
Pick it as you'd like

让咱吃一顿
And offer us a good meal

女：　莳菜已抽芽
Female：　Already in bud is Mbonq

莳菜已长高
Tall enough it grows

哥嫌老不要
Old leaves I don't pick

让咱能多吃几顿
More meals for young Mbonq

男：　莳菜嫩才要
Male：　Tender Mbonq would be fine

莳菜老就放

Old Mbonq not to take

让它长成藤

Leave it grow into vine

用它来缠耙

Harrow with it I'd make

女： 莳菜嫩才要

Female： Tender Mbonq would be fine

莳菜老就放

Old Mbonq not to take

让它长成藤

Leave it grow into vine

拿它来编筐

Basket with it I'd make

男： 二三月莳菜

Male： Mbonq in lunar February and March

吃两餐就厌

Two meals enough is enough

不像园中菜

Unlike vegetables in the field

餐餐吃不厌

Every meal far from enough

女: 二三月莳菜

Female: Mbonq in lunar February and March

餐比餐好吃

One meal better than the other

丢弃园中菜

Vegetables are put aside

相争吃野菜

Eager to go for potherb

男: 天天吃莳菜

Male: Mbonq for meals every day

餐比餐臭青

Fed up meal after meal[41]

咱再说别种

Not plant it any longer

咱找第二棵

Another potherb I'd hunt

女: 天天吃莳菜

Female: Mbonq for meals every day

餐比餐臭青

Fed up meal after meal

说别棵了哥

Something new we'd hunt

吃餐把竹笋

Why not some bamboo shoots?

男： 二三月开初

Male： Beginning of lunar February and March

竹笋别出土

Bamboo has been in sprout

我俩出去找

We'd out for searching

人早已占完

All has been taken out

女： 二三月开初

Female： Beginning of lunar February and March

竹笋别出土

Bamboo has been in sprout

我俩出去找

We'd out for searching

占这还有那

Take home all is left

男： 二三月找笋

Male： Lunar February and March for bamboo shoots

笋刚冒出土

They begin to spring up

妹你过去采

You go for them my dear

拿来我们吃

Take home for our meals

女：　　二三月找笋

Female： Lunar February and March for bamboo shoots

笋早已出土

Already they have sprung up

你慢过去要

You go for them my dear

拿来给咱吃

Take home for our meals

男：　　得吃节嫩笋

Male： Tender shoots I would like

又想吃辣笋

Spicy shoots I'd like too

凹地笋难找

Hard to find them in the valley

山上笋好寻

Good place on the mountain

女：　　得吃节嫩笋

Female： Tender shoots I would like

又想吃辣笋

Spicy shoots I'd like too

凹地笋难找

Hard to find them in the valley

山上笋难寻

So is on the mountain

男： 二三月找笋

Male： Lunar February and March for bamboo shoots

得两支细笋

Two slender shoots I've got

得两节甜笋

Two sweet shoots I've got

拿来供三月

Take home worship for lunar March

女： 二三月找笋

Female： Lunar February and March for bamboo shoots

得两支直笋

Two straight shoots I've got

得两节甜笋

Two sweet shoots I've got

拿来供祖先

Take home sacrifice for ancestors

男：　　二三月找笋
Male：　Lunar February and March for bamboo shoots

笋已高过娘
Shoots are taller than Mom

笋已长过顶
Over the head it grows

妹十九成娘
A mom of nineteen you become

女：　　二三月找笋
Female：Lunar February and March for bamboo shoots

笋已高过娘
Shoots are taller than Mom

笋下节先老
From the bottom it grows old

哥十五成爹
A dad of fifteen you become

男：　　先去的找笋
Male：　Early comers for bamboo shoots

后去的找筒
Late comers for bamboo tubes

找筒来做笛
Tubes for making a flute

给你满崽⁴²吹

For your little boy to play

女： 先去的找笋

Female： Early comers for bamboo shoots

后去的找筒

Late comers for bamboo tubes

找筒来做笛

Tubes for making a flute

给你长子吹

For your first boy to play

男： 青笋已近尾

Male： Bamboo shoots draw to an end

甜笋期将过

Sweet bamboo shoots would be past due

过笋期菜期

Season for shoots and vegetables out

妹去时已晚

Too late for your coming

女： 笋已渐脱壳

Female： Shoots have gradually peeled away

笋已渐过期

Bamboo shoot season comes to an end

过笋期花期
Season for shoots and vegetables is out

别费力去找
Searching for it is in vain

男： 找笋不得恋
Male： Searching for shoots or love

去恋不得笋
With either one I go home

找笋还能吃
Bamboo shoots could be eaten

我去恋空回
Searching for love it is in vain

女： 找笋不得恋
Female： Searching for shoots or love

去恋不得笋
With either one I go home

找笋还能吃
Bamboo shoots could be eaten

我去恋空回
Searching for love it is in vain

男： 圩日隔空日
Male： Rest interval of song fair days

快过风流时
Pass quicker than the days we meet

两日空又圩
Song fair comes after rest

过时悔不及
Pity it would be missed

女： 圩日连空日
Female： Rest interval of song fair days

两日空又圩
Song fair comes after rest

这时不风流
Delighted at singing songs

过时悔不及
Pity after it is passed

男： 过菜期笋期
Male： Season for vegetables and bamboo shoots out

妹去要还有
Some will remain for you

过了婚恋期
Once love season is over

死也不见妹
I can never see my lover

女： 过菜期笋期

Female： Season for vegetables and bamboo shoots is out

哥去要还有

Some will remain for you

过了婚恋朝

Once love season is over

再也挽不回

Never would love come back

男： 这菜期笋期

Male： Season for vegetables and bamboo shoots

有时很易过

So easily overdue it would be

不像年轻时

Unlike one at his young

日对三回歌

Sing three times a day

女： 这菜期笋期

Female： Season for vegetables and bamboo shoots

有时很易过

So easily overdue it would be

就是不过期

Even if it will never fade

谁知下辈怎么样

Who knows what will be?

采叶 Picking Leaves

男： 到二月廿七
Male： Lunar February the 27th comes

家家摘枫叶
Families are picking maple leaves

我没妻去摘
Having no wife to do it

叶还在山上
Maple leaves remain on the mount

女： 到二月廿七
Female： Lunar February the 27th comes

家家摘枫叶
Families are picking maple leaves

你有妻去要
Your wife will pick them

枫叶早到家
Back home with maple leaves

男： 山上有枫叶
Male： Maple leaves are on the mount

不要别人要
Others will pick them if you don't

明日才去要
If not pick them until tomorrow

别人早要光
None is left for you then

女： 山上有枫叶
Female： Maple leaves are on the mount

不要别人要
Others will pick them if you don't

情哥不去要
If you don't go for them

别人就要光
None is left for you then

男： 山上有枫叶
Male： Maple leaves are on the mount

不要别人要
Others will pick them if you don't

我也想去要
I'd like to pick them

别人早要光
None is left for me

女： 山上有枫叶
Female： Maple leaves are on the mount

不要别人要
Others will pick them if you don't

情哥不去要
If you don't go for them

真不剩到你
None is left for you then

男： 放到臼去舂
Male： Put it in a mortar and grind

放到椛去捣
Pound it with pestle in a bar

捣到楼外面
Make it outside the house

让子孙剥壳
Let the children learn to husk

女： 放到臼去舂
Female： Put it in a mortar and grind

放到椛去捣
Pound it with pestle in a bar

你有子有孙
Children and grandchildren you have

到晾台剥壳
On veranda they husk

男： 到二月廿八
Male： Lunar February the 28th comes

家家晾枫叶
Every family dries maple leaves

你妈真周到
Dilligent as your mom

最早拿来晾
The first one to dry them

女： 到二月廿八
Female： Lunar February the 28th comes

各家晾枫叶
Every family dries maple leaves

你爹真主动
Smart as your dad

比人早晾晒
To dry maple leaves earlier

男： 到二月廿八
Male： Lunar February the 28th comes

家家晾枫叶

Every family dries maple leaves

你的已在晒台晾

Yours are dried on the veranda

我的还长在林中

Mine remain on the mount

女： 到二月廿八

Female： Lunar February the 28th comes

家家晾枫叶

Every family dries maple leaves

你的已晾在晒台

Yours are dried on the veranda

我的还在树枝上

Mine remain on the branch

男： 到二月廿九

Male： Lunar February the 29th comes

人人采红蓝[43]

Gyaemq leaves that folks pick

个个浸枫叶

Maple leaves that folks steep

备染三月米

Ready to dye lunar March rice

女： 到二月廿九

Female：Lunar February the 29th comes

人人采红蓝

Gyaemq leaves that folks pick

个个浸枫叶

Maple leaves that folks steep

多色米难染

Different colors hard to dye

男： 到三月初一

Male：Lunar March the 1st comes

拿枫叶去泡

Maple leaves that folks steep

你泡在坛里

Yours steep in the jar

我的还飘在垌里

Mine remain on the mount

女： 到三月初一

Female：Lunar March the 1st comes

拿枫叶去泡

Maple leaves that folks steep

你妻真聪明

Smart as your wife

放到坛去浸

Steep them in the jar

男： 到三月初二

Male： Lunar March the 2nd comes

各处都捞鱼

Folks busy for catching fish

我无网无罾

No nets supported by stilts

钓得虾两只

Only two shrimps I've got

女： 到三月初二

Female： Lunar March the 2nd comes

各处都捞鱼

Folks busy for catching fish

你有网有罾

You have nets supported by stilts

捞得鱼得虾

Fish and shrimps I've got

男： 初二晚饭后

Male： After dinner on Lunar March the 2nd

拿枫叶来浸

Folks busy for steeping leaves

浸水慢火煎

Boiling them on small fire

拿箕来捞渣

With dustpans filtering residue

女： 初二晚饭后

Female： After dinner on Lunar March the 2nd

拿枫叶来浸

Folks busy for steeping leaves

夫锅边添火

Husband busy for feeding fire

妻用箕捞渣

Wife busy for filtering the residue

男： 枫叶要煎好

Male： Maple leaves will be ready

拿箕来捞渣

With dustpans filtering the residue

倒放大盆里

Pour leaf soup into a tub

捞不尽再滗

Fliter it again if it's not done

女： 枫叶要煎好

Female： Maple leaves will be ready

拿箕来捞渣
With dustpans filtering the residue

若渣捞不净
If leaf soup not clean

再用筛来算
With sieve filtering the residue

男：　咱煎好枫叶
Male：　Maple leaves will be ready

又去采红蓝
Gyaemq leaves that I pick

加上红蓝草
Mixed with the gyaemq leaves

红艳艳好看
Red color nice and bright

女：　咱煎好枫叶
Female：Maple leaves will be ready

又去采红蓝
Gyaemq leaves that I pick

加上红蓝草
Mixed with the gyaemq leaves

艳似嫂脸庞
Bright as your wife's face

男： 咱煎好枫叶
Male： Maple leaves will be ready

又去采黄花
Yaq leaves that I pick

加上香黄花
Mixed with fragrant yaq

染黄杂其中
Dyeing yellow in the rice

女： 咱煎好枫叶
Female： Maple leaves will be ready

又去采黄花
Yaq leaves that I pick

加上香黄花
Mixed with fragrant yaq

黄色更加艳
Yellow color nice and bright

男： 枫叶是枫叶
Male： Maple is maple

别贪要多色
No more colors you pick

不要爱多人
No more lovers you long for

弃旧人烂贱
The abandoned one looks poor

女： 枫叶是枫叶
Female： Maple is maple

染米要多色
If add more colors to dye

去恋爱多个
If long for more girls to love

背时是我俩
On us bad fortune'll befall

男： 煎枫叶染黑
Male： Maple leaves dye rice black

煎黄花染黄
Yaq leaves dye rice yellow

煎红草紫叶
Ci(j) and Se^{44} are dyeing rice

来染红染紫
In colors of red and purple

女： 煎枫叶染黑
Female： Maple leaves dye rice black

煎黄花染黄
Yaq leaves dye rice yellow

煎红草紫叶

Ci(j) and Se are dyeing rice

来染红染紫

In colors of red and purple

男： 傍晚吃过饭

Male： In the evening after dinner

都说去泡甑

Out for soaking rice steamer

把甑子泡好

Once the steamer's ready

明早蒸黑饭

Black rice steamed tomorrow morning

女： 傍晚吃过饭

Female： In the evening after dinner

都说去泡甑

Out for soaking rice steamer

把甑子泡好

Once the steamer's ready

才少费柴草

Only so could firewood be saved

男： 傍晚吃过饭

Male： In the evening after dinner

就拿米来泡
Take the rice to soak

拿米来浸泡
Put rice in the water

泡多少筒米
How much rice is fine?

女：　傍晚吃过饭
Female： In the evening after dinner

娘拿米来泡
Mom starts to soak rice

拿米来浸泡
Put rice in the water

十三筒才够
Thirteen tubes is just fine

男：　娘量来量去
Male： Mom keeps on measuring rice

倒进又倒出
Pouring rice in and out

又拿出几斤
Again she takes out some

留明年做种
Leave it as seeds for next year

女： 娘量来量去
Female：Mom keeps on measuring rice

倒进又倒出
Pouring rice in and out

又拿出几斤
Again she takes out some

留明年做种
Leave it as seeds for next year

男： 到三月初三
Male：Lunar March the 3rd comes

家家忙蒸饭
Families busy for steaming rice[45]

我家没有米
I have no sticky rice

黯然把火熄
Sadly I flameout the fire

女： 到三月初三
Female：Lunar March the 3rd comes

家家忙蒸饭
Families busy for steaming rice

你家有米多
More rice your family has

一早蒸两锅

You steam two pots tomorrow

男： 到三月初三

Male： Lunar March the 3rd comes

家家人齐齐

Family members are all here

齐似筒中筷

As chopsticks in the box

独我家叹气

Leave me sigh deeply at home

女： 到三月初三

Female： Lunar March the 3rd comes

家家人齐齐

Family members are all here

齐似筒中筷

As chopsticks in the tube

独我俩叹气

Leave us sigh deeply at home

男： 到三月初三

Male： Lunar March the 3rd comes

家家闹像官

Families bustle as county government

家家乱似州[46]

Families hustle as stae capital

独我家寂静

Lonely silence is in my home

女： 到三月初三

Female： Lunar March the 3rd comes

家家喜洋洋

Joy in every family

家家闹哄哄

Noisy in every house

只我家寂静

Only still in my home

男： 上家蒸十五

Male： A family steams rice 7.5 kg

下家蒸十四

B family steams rice 7 kg

我家蒸四两

We have only 0.2 kg

不够分子孙

Not enough for children to eat

女： 有多的多蒸

Female： Rich families steam more rice

有少的蒸少
Poor families steam less rice

我家呢蒸薯
Only sweet potatoes I steam

拿它去扫墓
To sweep ancestors' graves with them

男：　到三月初三
Male： Lunar March the 3rd comes

上屋爹蒸黑[47]
Dad steams black rice at backyard

每家分一坨
A piece of it each family gets

合拿去扫墓
To sweep ancestors' graves with it

女：　到三月初三
Female： Lunar March the 3rd comes

上屋伯蒸紫
Uncle steams purple rice at the front room

每家得一团
A piece of it each family gets

也够去扫墓
To sweep ancestors' graves with it

男： 糯饭乌
Male： With the black sticky rice

拿锄去铲墓
Take a hoe to shovel the grave

铲墓要女儿
I go for shovel so daughter stays

来替娘守屋
She stays at home instead of her mom

女： 糯饭乌
Female： With the black sticky rice

拿锄去铲墓
Take a hoe to shovel the grave

铲墓要女儿
I go for shovel so daughter stays

天天打丝绣
Making silk embroidery every day

男： 糯饭乌
Male： With the black sticky rice

拿锄去铲墓
Take a hoe to shovel the grave

铲墓要男儿
I go for shovel so son stays

去替爹犁田

Go plow the field for dad

女： 糯饭乌

Female： With the black sticky rice

拿锄去铲墓

Take a hoe to shovel the grave

铲墓要男儿

I go for shovel so son stays

成秀才跟官[48]

Be a scholar and official

男： 糯饭黑

Male： With the black sticky rice

扛锄去扫墓

Take a hoe to shovel the grave

扫过一处又一处

From one grave to another

初三日扫墓

On the 3rd of lunar March

女： 糯饭黑

Female： With the black sticky rice

扛锄去扫墓

Take a hoe to shovel the grave

扫过一处又一处

From one grave to another

初五日扫墓

On the 5th of lunar March

男： 到三月初四[49]

Male： Lunar March the 4th comes

邀同伴去玩

Inviting friends out to play

玩过一山山

From one mount to another

哪山合对歌

Where sing in antiphoral style

女： 到三月初四

Female： Lunar March the 4th comes

邀同伴去玩

Inviting friends out to play

玩过一坡坡

From one mount to another

莫圩合对歌

In Haw Mo(z) we'd go to sing

男： 到三月初四

Male： Lunar March the 4th comes

踊跃去莫圩

Rush to sing in Haw Mo(z)

一起到山上

Together we climb up a mount

箩跟鞋交换

Exchange basket for the shoes

女： 到三月初四

Female： Lunar March the 4th comes

踊跃来莫圩

Rush to sing in Haw Mo(z)

一起到山上

Together we climb up a mount

鞋跟箩交换

Exchange shoes for the basket

男： 蒸紫是蒸紫

Male： Purple is purple

不能比紫黑

Could not be darker than purple

紫黑在中间

Rice with purple black amid

五色饭扫墓

Five-color rice for sweeping graves

女： 蒸紫是蒸紫
Female： Purple is purple

不能比紫黑
Could not be darker than purple

紫黑紫泅泅
Rice with purple black amid

崽拿去扫墓
For the child to sweep graves

男： 有肥料的人[50]
Male： The family with dishes nice

糯饭软香甜
Rice soft, sweet with good smell

有子有孙人
With children and grandchildren at your side

有说又有笑
You all talk and laugh

女： 有肥料的人
Female： The family with dishes nice

糯饭软香甜
Rice soft, sweet with good smell

你有妻子在身边
Your wife is at your side

就忘前人传的歌
Songs of an old friend you forget

男： 有鱼有肉人
Male： Folks with fish and meat

把坟墓填高
Tombs are filled up high

我没有两菜
I have no dishes

弃荒坟不扫
The abandoned grave left lonely

女： 有鱼有肉人
Female： Folks with fish and meat

把坟墓堆大
Tombs are filled up large

我家苦又穷
I am poor without food

弃荒冢不扫
The abandoned grave left lonely

男： 闻鼓声下坳
Male： Hearing drums down to the hollow

咱到山背听
Listen to singing on the slope

鼓声下平地

Drums down to the ground

知妹家安龙

Knowing your family's burial

女： 闻鼓声下坳

Female： Hearing drums down to the hollow

咱到山背听

Listen to singing on the slope

鼓声下平地

Drums down to the ground

知哥家安龙

Knowing your family's burial

男： 闻鼓声下坳

Male： Hearing drums down to the hollow

咱到田边看

Seeing at the field side

鼓响田那边

Over the fields drums go

知妹家安龙

Knowing your family's burial

女： 闻鼓声下坳

Female： Hearing drums down to the hollow

咱到田边看
Seeing at the field side

鼓响岩下田
Over the fields drums go

咱就过去听
Listening to drums over there

男： 清明到初三
Male： From Qingming to the 3rd

各家安龙地
Each family is busy for burial

富贵人家他才安
Rich family holds the ceremony

我家贫穷也就罢
Poorly I could not make

女： 清明到初三
Female： From Qingming to the 3rd

各家安龙地
Each family is busy for burial

富贵人家他才安
Rich family holds the ceremony

我家贫穷也就罢
Poorly I could not make

春忙 Busy Spring

男：　二三月春分[51]

Male：　Spring Equinox in lunar February and March

鸟儿分四界

Birds live in different parts

各自在一方

On one side or another

各在林鸣唱

Each sings song in the woods

女：　二三月春分

Female：　Spring Equinox in lunar February and March

鸟儿分四界

Birds live in different parts

鸟各在丛中

On one bush or another

鱼水中跳跃去

Fish playfully in the water jump

男： 二三月清明[52]

Male： Pure Brightness in lunar Lunar February and March

历书上来报

The lunar calendar announces that

二三月以后

After lunar February and March

哪个报春分

Spring Equinox who will tell?

女： 二三月清明

Female： Pure Brightness in lunar Lunar February and March

惊蛰上来报

Insects awaken and forecast solar term

二三月以后

After lunar February and March

鸟儿报春分

Spring Equinox birds tell

男： 二三月清明

Male： Pure Brightness in lunar February and March

听蛙鸣叫声

Croak of frogs is far away

每天一两声

One or two croaks a day

把咱心搅乱

Bother me I have no way

女： 二三月清明

Female： Pure Brightness in lunar February and March

听蛙鸣叫声

Croak of frogs is far away

每天一两声

One or two croaks a day

以为是哥声

Thought it was your voice

男： 二三月清明

Male： Pure Brightness in lunar February and March

听到寒哈声

Hanq hag[53] starts to sing

听见妹说话

Your voice is heard far away

想爬去相会

How much I long to meet you

女： 二三月清明

Female： Pure Brightness in lunar February and March

蛙鸣声悠扬

Melodious is the frogs' croak

听见哥说话
Your voice is heard far away

却不能一起
Can't get together we regret

男：　二三月清明
Male：Pure Brightness in lunar February and March

与情妹同坐
Sitting with you in delight

听妹说甜言
Kind words you just say

永远记心间
Be forever in my mind

女：　二三月清明
Female：Pure Brightness in lunar February and March

与情哥相见
Meeting with my sweetheart today

听情哥好言
Kind words you just say

记永年永世
Will never go away

男：　二三月谷雨
Male：Grain Rain in lunar February and March

人人理棉地

Time for folks to work in the cotton fields

各撒各的种

Each one sows and spreads

各找各的妹

Each one looks for his sweetheart

男： 二三月以后

Male： After lunar February and March

忙播秧种棉

Busy for planting rice and cotton

种棉种蓼蓝

Planting cotton and indigo knotweed

到哪能遇妹

Where my lover I can meet?

女： 二三月以后

Female： After lunar February and March

忙播秧种棉

Busy for planting rice and cotton

种棉种蓼蓝

Planting cotton and indigo knotweed

到哪去对歌

Where can I go for song?

男： 二三月以后
Male： After lunar February and March

蝶催人运肥
Butterflies urge people to deliver fertilizer

运过山过垅
Cross mount and over ridge

去种土官田
To work on chieftains' land

女： 二三月以后
Female： After lunar February and March

蝶催人运肥
Butterflies urge people to carry fertilizer

运过山过垅
Cross mount and over ridge

去种皇帝田
To work on emperor's land

男： 二三月以后
Male： After lunar February and March

各人各奔忙
Each one busy for his own

有的忙种田
Some work in his fields

有的忙送肥
Some busy for delivering fertilizer

女： 二三月以后
Female： After lunar February and March

各人各奔忙
Each one busy for his own

有的忙种田
Some work on his fields

有的忙种棉
Some busy for planting cotton

男： 二三月以后
Male： After lunar February and March

天上雷声新
Spring thunder booms in the sky

二三月立春
Beginning of Spring in lunar February and March

下雨响春雷
Rain and spring thunder sounds

女： 二三月以后
Female： After lunar February and March

天上雷声新
Spring thunder booms in the sky

二三月立春
Beginning of Spring in February and March

下雨春雷响
Rain and spring thunder sounds

男： 二三月以后
Male： After lunar February and March

彩蝶各纷飞
Butterflies go in different ways

各人各心事
Each one has his own worry

不得住娘家
Can't live in your parents'

女： 二三月以后
Female： After lunar February and March

彩蝶各纷飞
Butterflies go in different ways

各人各心事
Each one has her own worry

难放声对歌
Can't enjoy singing songs

男： 二三月以后
Male： After lunar February and March

执刀找棉地

With sickle for cotton work

棉地在哪里

Where is your cotton field?

让我跟去砍

Let me follow you to work

女： 二三月以后

Female： After lunar February and March

执刀找棉地

With sickle for cotton work

棉地在山脚

Cotton field's at mount foot

等情哥去砍

I'm waiting for your work

男： 二三月以后

Male： After lunar February and March

执刀找豆地

With sickle for bean work

豆地在哪里

Where is your bean field?

让我跟去砍

Let me follow you to work

女： 二三月以后
Female：After lunar February and March

执刀找豆地
With sickle for bean work

豆地在林边
Bean field's at the woods

等情哥去砍
I'm waiting for your work

男： 二三月以后
Male：After lunar February and March

执刀找禾地
With sickle for crop work

禾地在哪里
Where is your crop field?

让我跟去砍
Let me follow you to work

女： 二三月以后
Female：After lunar February and March

执刀找禾地
With sickle for crop work

禾地在岭脚
Crop field's at mount foot

等情哥去砍
I'm waiting for your work

男：　二三月谷雨
Male：　Grain Rain in lunar February and March

见妹拿棉种
You carry the cotton seeds

拿棉种去撒
Away to sow in the fields

到哪能见妹
Where my lover I can meet?

女：　二三月谷雨
Female：Grain Rain in lunar February and March

见哥拿豆种
You carry the bean seeds

拿豆种去撒
Away to sow in the fields

到塘边去等
Waitig for you at the pond

男：　春雷响了妹
Male：　Growling is the spring thunder

春雨飘了妹
Falling down the spring rain

人扛耙下田

Into the fields men carry harrows

我上山锄地

Up the hills I hoe fields

女： 春雷响了哥

Female：Growling is the spring thunder

春雨飘了哥

Falling down the spring rain

哥扛耙下田

Into the fields you carry harrow

我上山锄地

Up the hills I hoe fields

男： 细雨纷纷下

Male：Spring drizzl keeps falling down

犁杖还未修

My plough has not been mended

还未修犁杖

Not yet mended my plough

还未翻土块

Not yet digged my fields

女： 细雨纷纷下

Female：Spring drizzle keeps falling down

犁杖你已修

Your plough has been mended

你早修犁杖

Have already mended your plough

你早翻土块

Have already digged your fields

男： 耕牛多人家

Male： Families with oxen and buffaloes

下雨也不歇

Keep working in the rain

我家耕牛缺

With no ox nor buffalo

泄气睡街上

Sleep on streets in despair

女： 你家耕牛多

Female： Oxen and buffaloes you have

雨多也不歇

Keep working in the rain

我家耕牛缺

With no ox nor buffalo

睡到夜才起

I don't get up until midnight

男： 细雨纷纷下
Male： Spring drizzle keeps falling down

轭还在树上[54]
Yoke's still on the tree

细雨纷纷下
Spring drizzle keeps falling down

还忙于租牛
For renting cattle I'm busy

女： 细雨纷纷下
Female： Spring drizzle keeps falling down

轭还在树上
Yoke's still on the tree

细雨纷纷下
Spring drizzle keeps falling down

牛还在外家
Cattle are in your parents' I could see

男： 细雨纷纷下
Male： Spring drizzle keeps falling down

轭套还未修
Not yet mended the yokesleeve

还未修轭套
Yokesleeve has not been mended

还未修弓轭
Bow yoke has not been mended

女： 细雨纷纷下
Female：Spring drizzle keeps falling down

轭套你早整
Yokesleeve has already been mended

你早整轭套
You've mended the yokesleeve

你早整弓轭
You've mended the bow yoke

男： 细雨纷纷下
Male： Spring drizzle keeps falling down

拿绳去哪里
Where to go with rope?

细雨纷纷下
Spring drizzle keeps falling down

忙找牛耕犁
Look for an ox to plough

女： 细雨纷纷下
Female：Spring drizzle keeps falling down

拿绳去外家[55]
Carry rope to my in-law's

外婆[56]牛大把

Mom-in-law has many oxen

外公牛满栏

Dad-in-law has many buffalos

男：　知你爹牛空
Male：　Your dad's ox is free

知你兄牛闲

Your brother's is also free

有只把幼牛

Some calves they both have

借我用天把

Please lend me for days

女：　我爹还有牛
Female：　My dad has a spare ox

我兄牛也空

My brother's is also free

空两头幼牛

Two calves are available for you

怕你费力教

Fear you teach things the hard way

男：　求伯娘开门
Male：　Ask Aunt in mon's side to open door

求姑妈开栏

Ask Aunt in Dad's side to open cowshed

开栏到里面

Into the cowshed let's see

借哪头给我

Which calf you'd lend me?

女： 伯娘早开门

Female： Aunt has opened the door

姑妈早开栏

Aunt has opened the cowshed

开门到里面

Open the door and get inside

再慢慢挑选

Pick it up as you like

男： 四月使幼牛

Male： In April I use the calf

两手抓两绳

With two ropes in my hands

牛老拉上埂[57]

Pull it up to the ridge

真难办啊妹

Really hard to make it

女：　四月使幼牛
Female：In April I use the calf

两手抓两绳
With two ropes in my hands

牛老拉上埂
Pull it up to the ridge

不行要别的
Why not try another one?

男：　四月使幼牛
Male：　In April I use the calf

两手抓两绳
With two ropes in my hands

牛老拉上埂
Pull it up to the ridge

真太恼火了
It makes me angry and sad

女：　四月使幼牛
Female：In lunar April I use the calf

两手抓两绳
With two ropes in my hands

牛老拉上埂
Pull it up to the ridge

找银买新的

I'd rather buy a new one

男： 四月犁田忙

Male： In lunar April I am busy for plowing

犁行又一行

Line after line

到头又转回

Going and returning on and on

顾不上情妹

No time to care about you

女： 四月犁田忙

Female： In lunar April I am busy for plowing

犁行又一行

Line after line

到头又转回

Going and returning on and on

哥真太累了

You work so hard my dear

男： 四月多雨水

Male： Lunar April comes with much rain

妹引水下田

You lead water to the fields

夫妻去做工
You work with your husand

我空想白盼
Leave me dream in vain

女： 四月雨渐多
Female：Lunar April comes with much rain

哥引水下田
You lead water to the fields

你有妻有子
You have both wife and son

哪还想到我
No me in your mind

男： 四月水下田
Male： In lunar April water goes to the fields

无妻儿早起
Bachelor gets up early to help

即使起得早
Even if I get up early

也落后别人
Later than the others do

女： 四月水下田
Female：In lunar April water goes to the fields

你有妻早起[58]

Your wife gets up early

早起来吵吵

A lot of noises she made

扰老人睡觉

Waking up the sleeping elderly

男： 四月水下田

Male： In lunar April water goes to the fields

没妻儿挑水

No wife or son carries water for me

自挑水自吃

Carrying water for my own

不如众同伴

Not so lucky as other folks

女： 四月水下田

Female： In lunar April water goes to the fields

你有妻挑水

Your wife carries you water

挑水给你吃

Water for you to enjoy

你比别人美

You're luckier than other folks

男：　四月水下田
Male：　In lunar April water goes to the fields

没妻儿送饭
No one carries me lunch

饭菜没人送
No rice，no dishes

饿死谁知道
Who knows when I starve?

女：　四月水下田
Female：　In lunar April water goes to the fields

有妻儿送饭
Wife and son bring you meals

送饭又送菜
With both rice and dishes

妻会爱会疼
She loves and cares about you

男：　四月水下田
Male：　In lunar April water goes to the fields

没妻儿修沟
No wife or son fixes the ditch

修沟到田埂
Lead the ditch to the field ridge

真羡慕情妹

How much I envy you

女： 四月水下田

Female：In lunar April water goes to the fields

妻和儿修沟

Wife and son fix the ditch

修沟又整埂

Fix the ditch and the field ridge

很羡慕情哥

How much I envy you

男： 有妻有儿人

Male：Folks with wife and son

田埂光似崖

Keep the field ridge clean

我俩无妻儿

I have no wife nor son

田埂多杂草

More grass on the field bank

女： 有妻有儿人

Female：Folks with wife and son

田埂光过人

Field bank cleaner than others'

我单身一人
I have no husband nor son

田埂草青青
Green grass on the field bank

男： 四月到立夏
Male： In lunar April comes Beginning of Summer

家家泡谷种
Every family soaks rice seeds

每家一二斤
One half or one kilo

拿到塘浸泡
Soak them in the pond

女： 四月到立夏
Female： In lunar April comes Beginning of Summer

家家泡谷种
Every family soaks rice seeds

每家一二斤
One half or one kilo

放水里浸泡
Soak them in the pond

男： 四月到初一
Male： Here comes April the 1st

拿谷种去泡
Every family soaks rice seeds

谷种泡水里
They soak them in water

久不久去看
Have a look once in a while

女： 四月到初一
Female：Here comes lunar April the 1st

拿谷种去泡
Every family soaks rice seeds

谷种泡水里
They soak them in the water

不久就成播
Going to sow soon after

男： 到四月初一
Male： Here comes lunar April the 1st

拿谷种去播
I start to sow the seeds

均匀播下地
Sow in the fields evenly

七天一片绿
In seven days they turn green

女： 到四月初一

Female： Here comes lunar April the 1st

拿谷种去播

I start to sow the seeds

均匀播下地

Sow in the fields evenly

七天就变绿

In seven days they turn green

男： 秧似针了妹

Male： Rice seedlings is in the ear

棯结蕾了友

Myrtle bushes sprout some buds

秧青幽田间

Seedlings in the fields grow green

棯花开山上

Myrtles are in full bloom uphill

女： 秧似针了哥

Female： Rice seedlings begin to ear

棯结蕾了友[59]

Myrtle bushes sprout some buds

棯花开山上

Myrtles are in full bloom uphill

等情哥去赏
Waiting for you to enjoy

男： 秧似针了妹
Male： Rice seedlings begin to ear

有妻人去撒
Other's wife goes to sow

秧一撒就长
So well the seedlings grow

不久就成拔
Could be lifted soon

女： 秧似针了哥
Female： Rice seedlings begin to ear

你有妻去播
Your wife goes to transplant them

秧一播就长
So well the seedlings grow

十五就成插
Lunar April the 15th they will be transp lanted

男： 水已满秧田
Male： Water has filled the seedling fields

大田水已满
Fields are full of water

水满下满上
Water is here and there

忙找人来插
Looking for hands to help me transplant the seedlings

女: 水已满秧田
Female: Water has filled the seedling fields

大田水已满
Fields are full of water

水满上满下
Water is here and there

你妻已去插
Your wife is already in the fields to transplant seedlings

男: 水秧三十四
Male: 34 days water rice grows

旱秧四十日
40 days dry rice does

秧成插了妹
After seedlings are transplanted

去垌或在家
You go for mount or at home

女: 水秧三十四
Female: 34 days water rice grows

旱秧四十日

40 days dry rice does

秧成插了哥

After seedlings are planted

但我没工做

I have no work to do

男： 秧苗青又壮

Male： Seedlings grow green and strong

秧壮正成扯[60]

Well enough to life them

心爱的情妹

My dear sweetheart

来帮扯几把

Please come and help

女： 秧苗青又壮

Female： Seedlings grow green and strong

秧壮正成扯

Well enough to life them

我想去帮扯

I'd like to come and help

怕被别人骂

But afraid of being blamed

男： 秧苗青又壮
Male： Seedlings grow green and strong

秧壮正成插
Well enough to be transplanted

心爱的情妹
My dear sweetheart

请来帮我插两把
Please come and help

女： 秧苗青又壮
Female： Seedlings grow green and strong

秧壮正成插
Well enough to be transplanted

我想去帮插
I'd like to come and help

怕人说去占
But afraid of being blamed

男： 妹扯秧就插
Male： Lift seedlings and you transplant them

我扯田边放
Lift them and put them aside

扯秧放田边
Lift them and put them aside

忙找人来插

Look for hands to help

女： 哥扯秧就插

Female：Lift seedlings and you transplant them

或扯了先放

Life them and put them aside

扯秧放田埂

Lift them and put them on the field banks

你妻跟耙插

After harrowing your wife transplant them

男： 有妻有儿人

Male： Folks with wife and son

秧插匀插满

Evenly and fully are seedlings transplanted

我无儿无妻

I have no son nor wife

田半空半插

Half done in my fields

女： 有妻有儿人

Female：Folks with wife and son

秧插匀插满

Evenly and fully are seedlings transplanted

你有妻有儿
You have wife and son

田早已插完
Fields have been well done

男： 有妻有儿人
Male： Folks with wife and son

秧插匀插满
Evenly and fully are seedlings transplanted

我无儿无妻
I have no son nor wife

田没有人插
No one helps to transplant them

女： 有妻有儿人
Female：Folks with wife and son

秧插匀插满
Evenly and fully are seedlings transplanted

哥有儿有妻
You have son and wife

秧插满插匀
Evenly and fully are seedlings transplanted

男： 人们忙插秧
Male： People are busy for transplanting seedlings

我刚教幼牛

I tame the calf just now

人插完又耘

Planting and weeding they busy for

我才忙扯秧

And I'm busy for lifting seedlings

女： 人们忙插秧

Female： Folks busy for transplanting seedlings

你摇扇游街

Hang out with a fan you instead

有妻插又耘

Planting and weeding your wife does

真快活了哥

So light-hearted you have been

男： 秧全已插完

Male： Seedlings have all been transplanted

田全已耘过

Fields have been well weeded

独哥那一丘

Only left undone in your fields

丢空在田里

Over there are empty fields

女： 秧全已插完
Female： Seedlings have all been transplanted

田全已耘遍
Fields have been well weeded

溪边的一片
The field by the brook

全被水冲光
Washed away by the flood

农事 Farm Work

男： 五月五
Male： It is lunar May the 5th

咱缺地少田
Short of field and land I'm

咱缺地少田
I'm short of field and land

拿啥配情妹
What do I have to please you?

女： 五月五
Female： It is lunar May the 5th

咱缺棉少布
Short of cotton and cloth I'm

咱少布缺棉
I'm short of cotton and cloth

哥空等空盼
Fear you expect in vain

男： 五月五
Male： It is lunar May the 5th

弃祖田不耕
Leaving the fields unplowed

弃官田不犁
Leaving the fields unploughed

去与妹对歌
Sing songs with my lover

女： 五月五
Female： It is lunar May the 5th

弃祖田不耕
Leaving the fields unplowed

弃官田不耘
Leaving the fields unploughed

去与哥对歌
Sing songs with my lover

男： 五月降大雨
Male： Heavy rain is falling in lunar May

水淹秧淹田
Seedlings and fields are all drown

如有妻起埂
Had I a wife to build the ridge

水似风过坳
Water runs as wind going through

女： 五月降大雨
Female：Heavy rain is falling in lunar May

水淹秧淹田
Seedlings and fields are all drown

夫和妻起埂
Husband and wife build the ridge

水似风过坳
Water runs as wind going through

男： 五月逢芒种
Male：Grain in Ear comes in Lunar May

水淹峎淹桥
Valleys and bridges are all drown

有妻与说笑
Talking and laughing with wife

热闹似鼓响
As joyous as beating a drum

女： 五月逢芒种
Female：Grain in Ear comes in Lunar May

水淹峎淹林
Valleys and woods are all drown

没有人来往
Nobody'd come and go

谢哥多照顾
It is very kind of you

男：　五月夏至到
Male：　Summer Solstice comes in Lunar May

已到耘田时
It's time to weed the fields

若能与妹配夫妻
Had I you as my wife

田早已耘光
All my fields would be weeded

女：　五月夏至到
Female：　Summer Solstice comes in lunar May

到了耘田时
It's time to weed the fields

有妻有子人
Folks with wife and son

田早已耘光
All the fields have been weeded

男：　六月六
Male：　Lunar June the 6th comes

水车还未扎

The waterwheel has not been tied

还未扎水车

Not been tied the waterwheel

怎么过牛节

How to spend the Ox Day

女： 六月六

Female： Lunar June the 6th comes

水车哥早扎

The waterwheel has been tied

哥已扎水车

You have tied the waterwheel

安心过牛节

Peace with it in the Ox Day

男： 六月六

Male： Lunar June the 6th comes

扎水车修戽

Tie waterwheel and fix scoop

从未在家吃顿饭

Never had a meal at home

心烦啰情妹

Being upset and nagging you

女：　六月六
Female：Lunar June the 6th comes

扎水车修戽
Tie waterwheel and fix scoop

顿顿在家吃好的
Eat good meals at home

哥你讥讽我
Brother you're mocking me

男：　六月六
Male：Lunar June the 6th comes

田干无法蹚
Fields too dry to tread on

田裂无法耘
Cracked fields can't be weeded

丢荒田垌里
A barren field it becomes

女：　六月六
Female：Lunar June the 6th comes

哥田早已蹚
Your fields have been done

七八个妯娌
Seven or eight sisters-in-law

相邀耘二遍
Come to weed a second time

男： 六月六
Male： Lunar June the 6th comes

田干无法耘
Fields too dry to be weeded

你那边人多
More hands you have there

耘田过初六
Lunar June the 6th comes

女： 六月六
Female： Lunar June the 6th comes

田未干先耘
Field is ploughed before it dries

耘来再耘去
Ploughing again and again

哥的禾苗好过人
Your rice looks better than others

男： 六月六
Male： Lunar June the 6th comes

田野绿油油
With green crops fields smile

我俩没有妻
We both are single without wife

禾苗半黄半变灰
Crops are half-yellow half-dry

女： 六月六
Female：Lunar June the 6th comes

田野绿油油
With green crops fields smile

你俩没有妻
You both have no wife

关咱什么事
It's no concern of mine

男： 六月逢小暑
Male：Minor Heat comes in lunar June

人人不在家
Everybody is not at home

一进入家门
On entering the house

人人喊口渴
Awful thirst everybody cries out

女： 六月逢小暑
Female：Minor Heat comes in lunar June

人人不在家
Everybody is not at home

一进入家门
On entering the house

人人都说困
Awful doze everybody cries out

男： 六月逢小暑
Male： Minor Heat comes in lunar June

到处禾苗青
With green crops fields smile

我俩身单个
We both are single without wife

活没完没了
Never-ending farm work in my life

女： 六月逢小暑
Female： Minor Heat comes in lunar June

到处禾苗青
With green crops fields smile

我俩啊单身
We both single without husband

单身人辛苦
Being single lives a hard life

男：　六月六
Male：　Lunar June the 6th comes

　　见人就捎话
　　Give my words to her

　　请妹过来玩
　　Here comes for joy and fun

　　不知能来不
　　Wondering if you would come

女：　六月六
Female：　Lunar June the 6th comes

　　不见人来喊
　　No one invites me to come

　　不喊自已去
　　If I come without invitation

　　人会怎么说
　　What the others would claim?

男：　七月逢立秋
Male：　Beginning of Autumn comes in lunar July

　　不说人不知
　　I know after somebody told

　　知那日立秋
　　Beginning of Autumn on that day I'd stay at home

都说不下田

No farm work would be made

女： 七月逢立秋

Female：Beginning of Autumn comes in lunar July

不说我不知

I know after somebody told

知那日立秋

Beginning of Autumn on that day I'd stay

咱在家绕纱

At home winding cotton yarns

男： 七月逢立秋

Male：Beginning of Autumn comes in lunar July

脚踩不到影

Dark shadow's hard to reach

弃蚊帐不挂

Mosquito nets are put aside

要花幔来盖

Brocades are needed in bed

女： 七月逢立秋

Female：Beginning of Autumn comes in lunar July

脚踩不到影

Dark shadow's hard to reach

弃蚊帐不挂
Mosquito nets are put aside

拿花幔来盖
Brocades are needed in bed

男： 七月逢立秋
Male： Beginning of Autumn comes in lunar July

日行渐南斜
Sun gradually turns southwards

夜长日渐短
Shorter days and longer nights

找长袖来穿
Long sleeve shirts I come to find

女： 七月逢立秋
Female： Beginning of Autumn comes in lunar July

日行渐南斜
Sun gradually turns southwards

夜长日渐短
Shorter days and longer nights

外需穿长袖
Long sleeve shirts I come to find

男： 七月逢立秋
Male： Beginning of Autumn comes in lunar July

田野禾抽穗

Rice in ear in the fields

先插或后插

Whenever transplanting seedlings

那时都抽穗

Will be in ear one day

女： 七月逢立秋

Female： Beginning of Autumn comes in lunar July

田野禾抽穗

Rice in ear in the fields

先插穗先出

The early be in ear

后插熟跟后

The late has to wait

男： 七月七

Male： Lunar July the 7th comes

提笠去看田

Bamboo hat I wear to the fields

稻刚勾似镰

Crops like sickles bowing down

回家典仓粮[61]

Home for fixing barn grain

女: 七月七
Female: Lunar July the 7th comes

忙着去看田
Busy for working in the fields

稻刚似牛尾
Crops like oxtails bowing down

回家开旧粮[62]
Home for fixing stored grain

男: 七月逢十四
Male: Lunar July the 14th comes

我叹气多多
Sadly I sigh a lot

没糯米祭祖
No sticky rice for ancestors

用啥过十四
How to make ancestor worship?

女: 七月逢十四
Female: Lunar July the 14th comes

哥叹什么气
What are you sighing for?

有糯米祭祖
With sticky rice for ancestor

扁糍供十四
Glutinous rice cakes as offerings

男： 七月逢十四
Male： Lunar July the 14th comes

托去赶圩的
Those go for folk fair

帮买二两油[63]
Help me with some oil

拿来点十四
To light up the altar

女： 七月逢十四
Female： Lunar July the 14th comes

托人买点油
I have some oil bought

点灯照神案
To light up the altar

点灯亮神台
To light up the niche

男： 七月逢十四
Male： Lunar July the 14th comes

人人剪冥衣
Everybody busy for making paper dresses

连穷人富人

No matter the rich or the poor

为祖先剪衣

Cut paper dresses for ancestors

女： 七月逢十四

Female：Lunar July the 14th comes

人人剪冥衣

Everybody busy for making paper dresses

穷的剪少点

The poor make fewer dresses

富家剪成堆

The rich make heaps of suits

男： 七月逢十四

Male：Lunar July the 14th comes

早早就祭祀

Doing worship as early as possible

有子有孙的

Folks with children and grandchildren

祭毕早吃饭

Having lunch after worship done

女： 七月逢十四

Female：Lunar July the 14th comes

早早就祭祀

Doing worship as early as possible

你有子有孙

Folks with children and grandchildren

祭毕早吃饭

Having lunch after worship is done

男：　到七月十四

Male：　Lunar July the 14th comes

个个有神佑

Every one has been blessed

有谁穷似我

Who is poor as me?

吃坡上楤果

Myrtles as my food on the slope

女：　到七月十四

Female：　Lunar July the 14th comes

个个有神佑

Every one has been blessed

有谁穷似我

Who is poor as me?

靠楤果养命

Living a life with myrtles

男： 七月逢十四

Male： Lunar July the 14th comes

人人有神护

Every one has been blessed

有谁穷像我

Who is as poor as me?

十四没两餐

No meals for the Day[64]

女： 七月逢十四

Female： Lunar July the 14th comes

人人有神护

Every one has been blessed

有谁穷像我

Who is as poor as me?

没两餐也过

Living a life without meals

男： 七月逢十四

Male： Lunar July the 14th comes

窜地边找笋

Searching uphill for bamboo shoots

有谁穷像我

Who is poor as me?

找笋供十四
Bamboo shoots for the Day

女： 你岳母有钱
Female： Your mom-in-law is wealthy

你岳父银多
Your dad-in-law is rich

分一坨给你
To give you some money

足够你买鸭
Buying ducks for the Day

男： 到七月十四
Male： Lunar July the 14th comes

稻不抽穗也扬花
Crops either in the ear or blossom

上下的田块
All over the paddy fields

稻不抽穗花也扬
Crops either in ear or blossom

女： 到七月十四
Female： Lunar July the 14th comes

禾苗全抽穗
Seedlings are all in the ear

连糯谷粳谷
Sticky rice and japonica rice

全都勾了头
Both are already in the ear

男：　稻日渐成熟
Male：　Rice comes to be ripe

棯日渐变紫
Myrtle comes to be purple

此茬稻成收
This crop of rice is harvested

问妹要新衣
Ask you for my new shirt

女：　稻日渐成熟
Female：　Rice comes to be ripe

棯日渐变紫
Myrtle comes to be purple

此茬稻成收
This crop of rice is harvested

问哥要新笠
Ask you for my new hat

男：　八月逢白露
Male：　White Dew comes in lunar August

禾苗全抽穗

Seedlings are all in the ear

不抽的就瘪

Shriveled husks not in the ear

不瘪的也枯

Having either shriveled or withered

女： 八月逢白露

Female：White Dew comes in lunar August

禾苗全抽穗

Seedlings are all in the ear

不抽的就瘪

Shriveled husks not in the ear

不瘪的也枯

Having either shriveled or withered

男： 八月逢白露

Male： White Dew comes in lunar August

开始尝新谷

New rice is all set

下边到上边

All over the village

家家尝青谷

Every family tries fresh rice

女：　　八月逢白露
Female：White Dew comes in lunar August

开始尝青谷
New rice is all set

下边到上边
All over the village

你家首先尝
Your family tries it first

男：　　到八月十五
Male：Lunar August the 15th arrives

转脸向火塘
Turn your face to the hearth

你爹有美酒
Your dad has good wine

烤火饮佳酿
Warmed by drinking around the fire

女：　　到八月十五
Female：Lunar August the 15th arrives

转脸向火塘
Turn your face to the hearth

你爹有美酒
Your dad has good wine

烤火饮佳酿

Warmed by drinking around the fire

男： 八月逢中秋

Male： Mid-Autumn Festival arrives in lunar August

与妹同赏月

Enjoying moon and sitting by your side

赏月吃月饼

With mooncakes we both share

保佑你成根[65]

Blessed you'll have a child

女： 八月逢中秋

Female： Mid-Autumn Festival arrives in lunar August

与哥同赏月

Enjoying moon and sitting by your side

赏月吃月饼

With mooncakes we both share

保佑你成爹

Blessed you'll have a child

男： 八月逢中秋

Male： Mid-Autumn Festival arrives in lunar August

与妹同赏月

Enjoying the moon and sitting by your side

赏月吃柚子

With pomelos we both share

不熟的不吃

We eat those nice and ripe

女： 八月逢中秋

Female：Mid-Autumn Festival arrives in lunar August

与哥同赏月

Enjoying the moon and sitting by your side

赏月吃橘子

With oragnges we both share

不好的不挑

We eat those ripe and nice

男： 八月逢秋分

Male：Autumnal Equinox comes in lunar August

谷种撒下田

In the fields seeds sowed

先种的齐肩

The early's grown to shoulder height

我后种平脚

Mine's late at the foot height

女： 八月逢秋分

Female：Autumnal Equinox comes in lunar August

谷种撒下田

In the fields seeds sowed

哥先种有收

Planted early you get harvest

我后种无获

But late work I get nothing

男： 八月逢秋分

Male： Autumnal Equinox comes in lunar August

拿禾剪下田

In fields with a sickle

稻刚像牛尾

Rice ears bowing down like oxtails

看情妹先剪

With a sickle you cut rice

女： 八月逢秋分

Female： Autumnal Equinox comes in lunar August

拿禾剪下田

In fields with a sickle

稻刚像牛尾

Rice ears bowing down like oxtails

回家舂陈谷

Stored rice home for pound

男： 九月九
Male： Lunar Septermber the 9th comes

采青谷来捋
I pick and thresh green rice

会捋不会舂
Can thresh but not pound

吃连糠带壳
Eating with bran and husk

女： 九月九
Female： Lunar Septermber the 9th comes

采青谷来捋
I pick and thresh green rice

夫捋妻来炒[66]
Your wife cooks it for dinner

我都闻到香
Mouth watering as it smells nice

男： 九月九
Male： Lunar Septermber the 9th comes

青谷晾在牛柱上
Green rice dries on the stand

我们俩单身
We both are single

青谷堆门口

Stacking it up on the ground

女： 九月九

Female： Lunar Septermber the 9th comes

青谷晾架上

Green rice dries on the stand

你妻真妖精[67]

How smart is your wife

鸡油炒青谷

With oil and green rice she fries

男： 九月九

Male： Lunar Septermber the 9th arrives

人人登高山

Great mountain every one climbs

有的在山腰扫墓

Some do tomb-sweeping at the hillside

有的采山枫

Some do maple-picking on the other side

女： 九月九

Female： Lunar Septermber the 9th arrives

人人登高山

Great mountain every one climbs

连主人仆人
Both master and his servants

登高山招手
Waving with others on hilltop

男： 九月逢大旦
Male： In September busy season comes

备担杆禾剪
Shoulder pole and sickles done

备禾剪给妹剪禾
Sickles to cut grains for you

修杆给妹挑禾把
Shoulder pole to carry grains for you

女： 九月逢大旦
Female： In September busy season comes

备担杆禾剪
Shoulder pole and sickles done

禾剪有人帮剪禾
Sickles ready to cut grains

担杆有人挑禾把
Shoulder pole to carry grain

男： 九月逢大旦
Male： In September busy season comes

扁担不离肩

Shoulder pole on my shoulders

担子不离手

Holding it in my hands

常站在山峁

In the valley I often stand

女： 九月逢大旦

Female： In September busy season comes

扁担不离肩

Shoulder pole on my shoulders

担子不离手

Holding it in my hands

日夜站峁里

In the valley I often stand

男： 九月逢大旦

Male： In September busy season arrives

夫和妻相拜

Huasband soon marries his wife

相拜又相夺

Marrying and fighting with each other

弃姑母分爨[68]

From aunt we live separate life

女： 九月逢大旦

Female： In September busy season arrives

夫和妻相拜

Huasband soon marries his wife

相拜又相踢

Marrying and fighting with each other

弃大妈分爨

From aunt we live separately

男： 九月逢大旦

Male： In September busy season comes

夫和妻备担

Ready for load the couple

担子像小船

Which looks like a boat

夫妻盘上肩

On shoulders are their tasks

女： 担子像小船

Female： The load's like a boat

夫妻盘上肩

Tasks on their shoulders

马儿往后退

Horse is scared and steps backward

夫打妻又拉
Whip and pull it they go home

男： 九月九
Male： Lunar Septermber the 9th comes

去府打陀螺
Out for spinning the top

打陀螺回来
Back home after playing

饭里全沾沙
The meal is stained with sand

女： 九月九
Female： Lunar Septermber the 9th comes

去府打陀螺
Out for spinning the top

牛残踏稻田
Cattle trample the rice fields

说又怕惹事
But how dare you to stop them

男： 禾断任它断
Male： Let it be for the broken grains

已有禾断顶
Over broken grains cry in vain

或有块把好

Or there are some other nice ones

明早咱来收

Tomorrow I come to reap them

女： 还有块把田

Female：There are some other fields

明早帮你收

Tomorrow I help you reap

帮你收明早

I help you reap tomorrow

你妻说咱次

Would your wife blame me?

男： 九月禾剪完

Male： September sees farm work done

十月田已空

Fields are empty when lunar October comes

田收空收尽

Farm work has been completed

坐等情妹来

Waiting for my lover come

女： 九月禾剪完

Female： Lunar September sees farm work done

十月田已空
Fields are empty when lunar October comes

田空人也闲
Farm work has been completed

去外面对歌
Outdoor we'd sing songs

男： 十月逢立冬
Male： Beginning of Winter comes in lunar October

想妹就去玩
Missing you I'd at your home

玩到妹那里
But when I go to hers

她已去夫家
She has been in husand's home

女： 十月逢立冬
Female： Beginning of Winter comes in lunar October

盼哥过来玩
Long to see you at home

盼初一十五
Expecting you day and night

都不见哥面
But I can't see you come

男： 十月十

Male： Lunar October the 10th arrives

家家备茶酒

Families prepare tea and wine

没兄弟朋友

Without brothers nor friends

空备办酒茶

Waiting somebody but in vain

女： 十月十

Female： Lunar October the 10th arrives

家家备茶酒

Families prepare tea and wine

没兄弟朋友

Without brothers nor friends

想不想喝酒

Wanna a cup of wine?

男： 十月北风寒

Male： In lunar October north wind blows hard

靠干柴取暖

Warm myself with firewood burned

怎样度过年

How to spend New Year?

穿啥度过冬

What to wear to resist cold?

女： 十月劲风吹

Female： In lunar October north wind blows cold

用竹篙拍棉

Beating cotton with a pole

穿棉衣过年

Cotton-padded clothes for New Year

盖棉被过冬

With a quilt winter be covered

男： 十月凉风起

Male： In lunar October north wind blows cold

遍地冻白霜

Ground is covered with frost

我缺衣少裤

Short of coats and pants I am

怎样度腊月

How to spend lunar December

女： 白衫衬棉袄

Female： White shirts and cotton-padded coats

你哪怕冻霜

Why are you afraid of frost?

富者配穷人
The rich and the poor

你哪知我俩
Both of us you know

男：　眼看年快到
Male： Chinese New Year's coming soon

草鞋无一双
No a pair of straw sandals

年快到了妹
Chinese New Year's coming soon

身上无分文
No a penny on my hand

女：　年快到了哥
Female： Chinese New Year's coming soon

衣带无一件
No a new dress on my closet

年快到了哥
Chinese New Year's coming soon

鞋袜无一双
No a pair of shoes nor socks

过年 Chinese New Year

男： 到腊月廿三
Male： Lunar December the 23rd arrives

人说是小年
People call it Little New Year

送灶王上天
Stove king was sent to the heaven

到除夕才回
Not return until Chinese New Year's Eve

女： 到腊月廿三
Female： Lunar December the 23rd arrives

人说是小年
People call it Little Chinese New Year

送灶王上天
Stove king was sent to the heaven

到除夕才回
Not return until Chinese New Year's Eve

男： 到腊月廿七
Male： Lunar December the 27th comes

家家剪粽叶
Bamboo leaves every family cuts

剪大叶小叶
Make them big or small

包大粽过年
For Chinese New Year big Zongzis are wrapped

女： 到腊月廿七
Female： Lunar December the 27th comes

家家剪芦叶
Reed leaves every family cuts

芦叶也没有
Without reed leaves I go

上山找枉叶
Vangh leaves uphill to find

男： 到腊月廿八
Male： Lunar December the 28th arrives

家家杀大猪
Big pig every family kills

连穷人财主
Both the poor and the rich

都杀猪过年[69]
Kill pigs for Lunar New Year

女： 到腊月廿八
Female：Lunar December the 28th arrives

家家杀大猪
Big pig every family kills

连贫穷人家
Even the poor family

也分肉下担
Gets a piece of pork

男： 到腊月廿九
Male： Lunar December the 29th arrives

人人买新衣
New clothes every one buys

买新衣装扮
Dressed up with new clothes

好像要出阁
As if she's ready to marry

女： 到腊月廿九
Female：Lunar December the 29th arrives

见你买新衣
See you buy new clothes

买新衣花衣

New flower clothes you'd buy

像是送给妻

Are they for your wife?

男：　到腊月廿九

Male：Lunar December the 29th arrives

见妹添新被

See you buy new quilts

添新被过冬

New quilts for winter

丢弃同不顾[70]

Care about me you've no time

女：　到腊月廿九

Female：Lunar December the 29th arrives

见哥添新被

See you buy new quilts

添新被给妻

New quilts for your wife

丢弃咱不顾

Care about me you've no time

男：　到了除夕夜

Male：The New Year's Eve arrives

家家整香炉

Every family offers incense burner

连穷人仆人

Both the poor and the servants

整祖先香炉

Clean censers for ancestors

女： 到了除夕夜

Female： The New Year's Eve arrives

家家整香炉

Every family cleans incense burner

连穷人仆人

Both the poor and the servants

忙拾掇香炉

Clean censers for ancestors

男： 到了除夕夜

Male： The New Year's Eve arrives

忙拾掇香炉

Busy for cleaning their censers

今年是大年

A big year this year is

祖先要回来

Ancestors would all arrive

女： 到了除夕夜
Female： The New Year's Eve arrives

忙拾掇香炉
Busy for cleaning their censers

今年是大年
A big year this year is

祖先下来坐
Ancestors would all arrive

男： 富人香炉大
Male： Censers are big in the rich households

穷人香炉小
Censers are small in the poor households

牌位无处贴
No place to paste tablet

贴篱上了事
On fence I put them

女： 你富香炉大
Female： Censers big in your home

咱穷香炉小
Censers small in my home

神牌无处贴
No place to paste tablet

贴篱上了事
On fence I put them

男： 到了除夕夜
Male： The New Year's Eve arrives

家家放鞭炮
Every family sets off firecrackers

鞭炮噼叭响
Crackling the firecrackers may sound

神仙降人间
The immortals come to earth

女： 到了除夕夜
Female： The New Year's Eve arrives

家家放鞭炮
Every family sets off firecrackers

鞭炮噼叭响
Crackling the firecrackers may sound

神仙下来坐
The immortals come to earth

男： 棵树十二枝
Male： A tree has twelve branches

只一枝修剪
Only one branch is pruned

一年十二晦[71]

12 last days in each year

只这晦欢乐

Only this offer is happy

女： 棵树十二枝

Female： A tree has twelve branches

只一枝修过

Only one branch is pruned

一年十二晦

12 last days in each year

只有这晦愁

Only the last day of a year worried

男： 到大年初一

Male： Chinese New Year's Day arrives

家家煮蛋洒

Every family would boil eggs

户户祭祖先

Every household worships ancestors

迎新年来到

The Chinese New Year is expected

女： 到大年初一

Female： Chinese New Year's Day comes

家家煮蛋洒

Every family would boil eggs

户户祭祖先

Every household worships ancestors

求千年平安

To pray being safe and sound

男： 新年头一天

Male： Lunar January the 1st comes

家家贴春联

Every family pastes Spring Festival couplets

春联贴门口

Spring Festival couplets on the door

求福又求寿

Pray for wealth and health they

女： 新春头一天

Female： Lunar January the 1st comes

家家贴春联

Every family pastes Spring Festival couplets

春联贴门口

Spring Festival couplets on the door

求早日发财

Pray for making big fortune

男：　正月头一天
Male：　Lunar January the 1st comes

邀妹去占卦
Invite you for drawing lot

占了一卦又一卦
One lot after another

看哪卦吉利
Which one is lucky lot?

女：　正月头一天
Female：　Lunar January the first comes

邀哥去占卦
Invite you for drawing lots

占了一卦又一卦
One lot after another

红卦是吉利
The red lot is a lucky one

男：　到正月初二
Male：　Lunar January the 2nd comes

一早就祭鬼
In the morning ancestors are honored

有子有孙人
Folks with children and grandchildren

祭鬼快吃饭

Have dinner after work's done

女： 到正月初二

Female：Lunar January the 2nd comes

一早就祭鬼

In the morning ancestors are honored

有子有孙人

Folks with children and grandchildren

祭鬼早吃饭

Have dinner after work's done

男： 正月初二日

Male： Lunar January the 2nd comes

你忙接礼担

Accepting gifts you've done

粽子大如臼

Zongzi's as big as a mortar

够吃好几餐

Big enough for several meals

女： 正月年初二

Female：Lunar January the 2nd it is

哥送肉送粽

Zongzi and meat you send me

糯粽大如斗
Zongzi's as big as a hat

足够你妻吃几餐
Big enough for several meals

男： 正月初三日
Male： Lunar January the 3rd it is

家家都请客
Every family makes a feast

请客又请酒
Present food and wine to guests

不来的去叫
Go for those who are absent

女： 正月初三日
Female： Lunar January the 3rd it is

家家都请客
Every family makes a feast

请客又请茶
Present food and tea to guests

全都请到齐
All invited to come and meet

男： 正月初四日
Male： Lunar January the 4th it is

叫契子都来

All adopted sons're asked to come

不论近或远

No matter near or far

全都叫来齐

All invited to come and meet

女： 正月初四日

Female： Lunar January the 4th it is

邀伙伴来聚

All friends're asked to come

连上面下面

Up and down the village

初四都来聚

All invited to come and meet

男： 到正月初五

Male： Lunar January the 5th it is

与兄弟抽签

With brothers I draw lots

一签又一签

One lot after the other

看哪签吉利

Which is a lucky lot?

女： 到正月初五
Female： Lunar January the 5th it is

替兄弟抽签
For my brother I draw lots

一签又一签
One lot after the other

看哪签吉利
Which is a lucky lot?

男： 到正月初六
Male： Lunar January the 6th it is

替情妹算卦
For my lover I draw lots

算卦又一卦
One lot after the other

问哪卦是吉
Which is a lucky lot?

女： 到正月初六
Female： Lunar January the 6th it is

替情哥算卦
For my lover I draw lots

算卦又一卦
One lot after the other

紫红那卦利

Amaranth is the lucky lot

男： 到正月初七

Male： Lunar January the 7th it is

争先去看戏

People rush to enjoy plays

去申圩⁷²看戏

Go to the fair for it

到黑岗相等

Wait for me at the hill

女： 到正月初七

Female： Lunar January the 7th it is

纷纷去看戏

People rush to enjoy plays

去心圩看戏

Enjoy plays at the fair

到黑岗对歌

Sing songs at the hill

男： 到正月初八

Male： Lunar January the 8th it is

人人刮火灰

Fire ash everyone collects

穷人或富人

The poor or the rich

刮火灰堆肥

Fire ash is collected for fertilizer

女： 到正月初八

Female： Lunar January the 8th it is

刮火灰堆肥

Fire ash is collected for fertilizer

我们没有肥

No fertilizer I have

刮火灰去撒

Fire ash is collected for the fields

男： 到正月初九

Male： Lunar January the 9th it is

家家热大粽

Big Zongzi has been heated

连贫穷人家

Even the poor has Zongzi

也吃大粽才运肥[73]

Only big Zongzi help do the labor

女： 到正月初九

Female： Lunar January the 9th it is

有粽的热粽
Folks heat Zongzi to eat

我们粽没有
We have no Zongzi but sweet-potatoes

吃完薯就去运肥
Deliver fertilizer after our meals

男： 到正月初十
Male： Lunar January the 10th it is

拾粽叶下河
Into the river for bamboo leaves

没妻拿去倒
I have no wife to do it

让前母替代
Old mom is asked to help me

女： 到正月初十
Female： Lunar January the 10th it is

拾粽叶下河
Into the river for bamboo leaves

你妻拿去倒
Your wife does it for you

让前妈安逸
Leave old mom at ease

男： 到正月十一
Male： Lunar January the 11th it is

情妹去婆家
You leave for your husband's

回家吃十五
To celebrate the Lunar January the 15th

等不到十四
Before the 14th arrives

女： 到正月十一
Female： Lunar January the 11th it is

你妻先回来
Your wife has been back

黄花[74]在哪里
Where are the yellow flowers?

让她先去采
Ask her to pick them

男： 到正月十二
Male： Lunar January the 12th it is

你四处巡山
You're patrolling around the mount

四处去寻花
Searching for flowers everywhere

高山变低山
Then high hill becomes low hill

女： 到正月十二
Female：Lunar January the 12th it is

你妻先巡山
Your wife patrols around hill

四处去寻花
Searching for flowers everywhere

高山变低山
Then high hill becomes low hill

男： 到正月十三
Male： Lunar January the 13th it is

家家晾黄花
Every family dries yellow flowers

哪家前天晾
The day before yesterday they were dried

全村寨香遍
Yellow flowers have perfumed the village

女： 到正月十三
Female：Lunar January the 13th it is

家家晒黄花
Every family dries yellow flowers

你妻前天晒

The day before yesterday they were dried

香遍全村寨

Your wife's flowers have perfumed the village

男： 到正月十四

Male： Lunar January the 14th it is

个个采黄花

Every family picks yellow flowers

明日到十五

Tomorrow will be the 15th

家家采黄花

Every family picks day lilies

女： 到正月十四

Female： Lunar January the 14th it is

个个托人去要花

Every one looks for flowers

明日到十五

Tomorrow will be the 15th

家家采黄花

Every family picks yellow flowers

男： 到正月十五

Male： Lunar January the 15th it is

家家采黄花

Every family picks yellow flowers

黄花在山上

Yellow flowers are on the hill

染黄饭色鲜

To dye rice yellow and bright

女： 到正月十五

Female： Lunar January the 15th it is

家家采黄花

Every family picks yellow flowers

黄花染黄饭

The flowers dye rice yellow

别火烧黄花

Do not burn the flowers

男： 到正月十五

Male： Lunar January the 15th it is

咱下去观灯

We go down for the lanterns

有先去后去

The early or the late comers

到城外休息

Take a rest outside the city

女： 到正月十五
Female： Lunar January the 15th it is

咱下去观灯
We go down for the lanterns

有先去后去
The early or the late comers

到楼下相等
Wait for me downstairs

男： 到正月十六
Male： Lunar January the 16th it is

家家收供桌
Every family puts altar away

连富人仆人
Both the rich and the servant

全都盼来年
Expecting the coming of the Chinese New Year

女： 到正月十六
Female： Lunar January the 16th it is

家家收供桌
Every family puts altar away

连富人仆人
Both the rich and the poor

都拼搏来年

Work hard for the coming of the Chinese New Year

男： 人家过年我也过

Male： Celebrate the Chinese New Year as the others do

偌大个年二两肉

A piece of pork for the Chinese New Year

二两猪肉过个年

Celebrate the Chinese New Year with it

多凄凉啊妹

What a life poor and dreary

女： 人家过年我也过

Female： Celebrate the Chinese New Year as the others do

偌大个年二两肉

A piece of pork for the Chinese New Year

凄凉就由它凄凉

Poor and dreary as it is

难道年会被卡住

Will the Chinese New Year be stopped?

期盼 Expectation

男： 过完年
Male： After the Chinese New Year

转眼到二月
Here comes lunar February

到二月十九
Lunar February the 19th comes

去交友游玩
Together we go and play

女： 过完年
Female： After the Chinese New Year

转眼到二月
Here comes lunar February

到二月十九
Lunar February the 19th comes

去和友对歌
Together we go and sing

男： 做人盼什么
Male： What do folks long for?

就盼玉米花
For the corn will bloom

大官盼主人
Chieftains long for being kings

我十分盼你
I long for meeting you

女： 做人盼什么
Female： What do folks long for?

就盼玉米花
For the corn will bloom

大官盼大王
Chieftains long for being kings

我真盼望你
I long for meeting you

男： 做人盼什么
Male： What do folks long for?

就盼小麦花
For the wheat will bloom

客人盼军人[75]
Cantonese Han long for Mandarine Han

我十分盼你

I long for meeting you

女： 做人盼什么

Female：What do folks long for?

就盼小麦花

For the wheat will bloom

客人盼军人

Visitors long for the soldiers

我盼你照顾

I long for your care

男： 人生盼什么

Male：What do folks long for?

就盼小米花

For the millet will bloom

小米花能吃

Millet flowers could be eaten

我能否盼你

May I long for meeting you?

女： 人生盼什么

Female：What do folks long for?

就盼小米花

For the millet will bloom

小米花能吃

Millet flowers could be eaten

我盼你照顾

I long for your care

男： 人生盼什么

Male： What do folks long for?

就盼旱禾花

For grain flowers in the farmland

天上盼地下

Sky longs for the earth

我非常盼你

I long for meeting you

女： 人生盼什么

Female： What do folks long for?

就盼旱禾花

For grain flowers in the farmland

天上盼地下

Sky longs for the earth

我盼你照顾

I long for your care

男： 人生盼什么

Male： What do folks long for?

盼崖顶青藤

For the ivy on the cliff

盼天上条根

For roots up in the sky

我真情盼你

How I long for my dear

女： 人生盼什么

Female： What do folks long for?

盼崖顶朵花

For the flower on the cliff

盼天上青藤

For the ivy in the sky

我盼你照顾

I long for your care

男： 燕子盼屋檐

Male： Swallows long for the eaves

鹧鸪盼水边

Partridges long for riverside

水边干涸了

Water runs dry on riverside

鸟到哪依靠

Where can the partridge stay?

女： 燕子盼屋檐

Female： Swallows long for the eaves

斑鸠盼水边

Partridges long for riverside

水边太迢遥

Water runs too far away

到哪找依靠

Where can the partridge stay?

男： 正月别盼神

Male： Don't expect gods in lunar January

神去吃香火

They have gone for incense

正月别盼哥

Don't expect me in lunar January

哥祭供祖先

Burning incense I pray for ancestors

女： 正月盼情哥

Female： Long for meeting you in lunar January

哥拜仙未回

You're out for burning incense

回不见就查

I check up your itinery

查不着就盼
I long for meeting you

男： 二月别盼花
Male： Don't expect flowers in lunar February

花正在含蕾
They are still in bud

二月别盼哥
Don't expect me in lunar February

哥在找棉地
I'm looking for cotton fields

女： 二月盼情哥
Female： Long for meeting you in lunar February

伙伴来就问
Asking your friends I meet

就查问啊哥
Ask them where you are

不见哥就盼
Missing you when out of sight

男： 三月别盼燕
Male： Don't expect swallows in lunar March

燕衔泥造窝
They are carrying mud to build nests

三月莫盼哥
Don't expect me in lunar March

哥做工没空
I'm busy in the fields

女： 三月盼情哥
Female：Long for meeting you in lunar March

像奔丧戴孝
As hurry home for the funeral

我盼你啊哥
I long for meeting you

不见哥就盼
Missing you when out of sight

男： 四月别盼蝶
Male： Don't expect butterflies in lunar April

蝶送肥下田
They're delivering fertilizer to the fields

四月别盼哥
Don't expect me in lunar April

哥正培旱禾
I'm busy planting seedlings

女： 四月盼情哥
Female：Long for meeting you in lunar April

个个来都问

Asking your friends I meet

我盼你啊哥

I long for meeting you

不见哥就盼

Missing you when out of sight

男： 五月别盼坝
Male： Don't expect dams in lunar May

坝拦水推车

They're working for the waterwheel

五月别盼哥

Don't expect me in lunar May

哥引水下田

I'm busy watering the fields

女： 五月盼情哥
Female： Long for meeting you in lunar May

真痛苦多多

Missing you I suffer a lot

我多么想你

How much I long for you

你车水没空

You're busy for the work

男： 六月别盼车
Male： Don't expect waterwheels in lunar June

车正转啰啰
They're busy turning to raise water

六月别盼哥
Don't expect me in lunar June

哥车水没空
I'm busy for watering the fields

女： 六月盼情哥
Female： I long for meeting you in lunar June

像雏鸟盼娘
As baby birds long for mom

像娘去赶圩
As mom goes for shopping

不见你就盼
Missing you when out of sight

男： 七月别盼蜂
Male： Don't expect bees in lunar July

蜂正忙采蜜
Bees are busy gathering honey

七月别盼我
Don't expect me in lunar July

我正忙灌田

I'm busy in watering the fields

女： 七月盼情哥

Female： Long for meeting you in lunar July

傍晚去引水

You still work at dark night

哥引水下田

Drawing water to the fields

不见面就盼

Missing you when out of sight

男： 八月别盼凤

Male： Don't expect phoenix in lunar August

凤仍在高山

It's flying up on the mount

八月别盼哥

Don't expect me in lunar August

哥累死累活

I'm tired and exhausted

女： 八月盼情哥

Female： Long for meeting you in lunar August

个个来都问

Ask your friends I meet

我盼你啊哥
I long for meeting you

久不见就盼
Missing you when out of sight

男： 九月别盼马
Male： Don't expect horses in lunar September

马去驮冬货
They're carrying cargoes for winter

九月别盼哥
Don't expect me in lunar September

哥做工没空
I'm busy for farm work

女： 九月盼情哥
Female： Long for meeting you in lunar September

谁来我都问
Ask whomever I meet

见不着就问
Ask them when you're out of sight

问不着就盼
Missing you with no answer

男： 十月别盼牛
Male： Don't expect cattle in lunar October

牛在田吃草
They're eating grass on hills

十月别盼哥
Don't expect me in lunar October

哥在数银钱
I'm busy for counting coins

女:　十月盼情哥
Female： Long for meeting you in lunar October

谁来我都问
Ask whomever I meet

问哥在不在
Ask them if you're home

久不见就盼
Missing you when out of sight

男:　冬月别盼羊
Male： Don't expect goats in lunar November

羊在崖吃草
They're eating grass on the hill

冬月别盼哥
Don't expect me in lunar November

哥崖上砍樵
I'm cutting woods on the cliff

女： 冬月盼情哥

Female：Long for meeting you in lunar November[76]

见亲戚就问

Ask my relatives I meet

真盼你啊哥

How I long for meeting you

久不见就盼

Expecting you when out of sight

男： 腊月别盼泉

Male：Don't expect the spring in lunar December

泉水清幽幽

Spring is deep and green

腊月别盼友

Don't expect friends in lunar December

友去交贩货

They go for exchanging goods

女： 腊月盼情哥

Female：Long for meeting you in lunar December

人来我就问

Ask whomever I meet

问这又问那
Ask them this and that

久不见就盼
Missing you when out of sight

节气 Solar Terms

男： 正月建寅月
Male： Lunar January is the month of Jianyin

设立春雨水
Both Beginning of Spring and Rain Water it has

到正月初二
Lunar January the 2nd comes

气温渐回升
It's warmer day by day

女： 去买姜来备
Female： Go to buy some gingers

不是种姜时
Not the right time to plant them

正月建寅日
Lunar January is the month of Jianyin

建立春雨水
Beginning of Spring and Rain Water it has

男： 二月建卯日
Male： Lunar February is the month of Jianmao

哪只报春分
To be Spring Equinox it has claimed

蝈蛩叫声急[77]
Gveng Gveiq sound so happily

各家种下地
Every one's busy growing crops

女： 拿小米来播
Female： Millet is sowed in the field

六月就收获
Harvest in June will be

二月建卯日
Lunar February is the month of Jianmao

鸟啼报春分
Spring Equinox heralded by birds singing

男： 三月建辰日
Male： Lunar March is the month of Jianchen

见清明谷雨
Pure Brightness and Grain Rain it has

无兄又无弟
No younger brothers nor elder brothers

四处无依靠

Nobody could I depend on

女： 要芋种来壅

Female： Taro is planted in this day

几时才长成

When will it grow ripe?

三月建辰月

Lunar March is the month of Jianchen

见清明谷雨

Pure Brightness and Grain Rain it has

男： 四建巳将过

Male： Lunar April is the month of Jiansi

立夏小满临

Beginning of Summer and Grain Buds here come

四月成插秧

Seedlings are transplanted in lunar April

十月忙收获

In October harvest will come

女： 四月需要雨

Female： Rain is needed in lunar April

需雨水下田

Water is needed in paddy fields

四建巳将过

Lunar April is the month of Jiansi

立夏小满临

Here come Beginning of Summer and Grain Buds

男： 五月五无用

Male： Lunar May the 5th comes

芒种夏至到

It's time for Grain in Ear and Summer solstice

五月无午饭

No lunch in lunar May

难迈步下田

Too hungry to work in fields

女： 听见蝉声喧

Female： Cicada singing in a noisy way

下田手脚软

Down to the fields I feel faint

五月五无用

Lunar May the 5th comes

芒种夏至临

It's time for Grain in Ear and Summer Solstice

男： 六建未了同

Male： Lunar June is the month of Jianwei

逢小暑大暑
Here come Minor Heat and Major Heat

大暑没有风
There's no wind in Major Heat

动辄满身汗
Be sweating all over easily

女： 两手拿两扇
Female： With fans in my hands

仍不见凉爽
Still not cool I feel

六月建未月
Lunar June is the month of Jianwei

逢小暑大暑
Here come Minor Heat and Major Heat

男： 七月建申月
Male： Lunar July is the month of Jianshen

入立秋处暑
Beginning of and End of Heat it has

处暑忌耕种
Farm work is tabooed in the End of Heat

有力也不耕
No plough even he's powerful

女：　七月逢十四
Female：Lunar July the 14th comes

窜田埂找吃
Search for food on ridges

七月建申月
Lunar July is the month of Jianshen

入立秋处暑
Here come Beginning of Autumn and End of Heat

男：　八月是建酉
Male：Lunar August is the month of Jianyou

白露和秋分
Here come White Dew and Autumn Equinox

连禾苗稗草
Both grain seedlings and barnyard grass

全都结了穗
All have put forth ears

女：　请情哥喝酒
Female：Invite you to drink wine

淡酒变烈酒
Light wine turns to be strong

八月酉要知
Lunan August is the month of Jinayou

白露与秋分
Here come White Dew and Autumn Equinox

男：　　九建戌了妹[78]
Male：　Lunar September is the month of Jianxu

寒露霜降临
Here come Cold Dew and Frost's Descent

连瓜果葫芦
Both gourds and melons

全都收回来
All are collected and carried home

女：　　九建戌了哥
Female：Lunar September is the month of Jianxu

寒露霜降临
Here come Cold Dew and Frost's Descent

连瓜果葫芦
Both gourds and melons

全都收回来
All are collected and carried home

男：　　十建亥了同[79]
Male：　Lunar October is the month of Jianhai

入立冬小雪
Here come Beginning of Winter and Minor Snow

凛冽北风起

The north wind blows chilly

人人换棉衣

Every one puts on paddy coat

女： 十月凉风起

Female： Lunar October cool wind blows

手不离棉团

Hands are kept inside my coats

十建亥了同

Lunar October is the month of Jianhai

入立冬小雪

Here come Beginning of Winter and Minor Snow

男： 一月建子日[80]

Male： Lunar November is the month of Jianzi

要给牛保暖

Time to keep the cattle warm

今年也很冷

It's really cold this year

牛不能出栏

Cattle have to stay indoors

女： 一建子了哥[81]

Female： Lunar November is the month of Jianzi

北风多回刮

North wind blows once again

北风刮凛冽

Strong north wind is rather cold

进大雪冬至

Here come Major Snow and Winter Solstice

男： 腊月建丑月

Male： Lunar December is the month of Jianchou

小寒大寒到

Here come Minor Cold and Major Cold

四月吃租粮

Folks borrow grain in lunar April

十月舀去还

And return it in lunar October

女： 腊月建丑月

Female： Lunar December is the month of Jianchou

小寒大寒到

Here come Minor Cold and Major Cold

到小寒大寒

When Minor Cold and Major Cold arrive

家家还租粮

Every family return rented grain

时辰 The Hour

男： 轻蘸墨写字
Male： Dip ink lightly to write characters

重蘸墨写对
Dip ink heavily to write couplets

情妹多知识
My lover is so intelligent

先起时辰歌
To start songs of the hour

女： 读诗书不伶
Female： Not clever in reading books

读经书不俐
Not smart in reading classics

子是什么时
What time is Zi?

你讲给我听
Would you please tell me?

男：　　子时是鼠时
Male：　Period of Mouse is Zi

鼠啃仓咬衣
Mouse gnaws at barns and clothes

嘴尖齿又利
With sharp mouth and teeth

偷吃油吃肉
Steal away oil and meat

女：　　读诗书不伶
Female：Not clever in reading books

读经书不俐
Not smart in reading classics

丑是什么时
What time is Chou?

你讲给我听
Would you please tell me?

男：　　丑时是牛时
Male：　Chou is the Period of Cattle

绳牵去犁地
Head for field to plough

细雨下沥沥
Drizzle keeps falling down

它仍去拉耙
Cattle still keep working hard

女： 读诗书不伶
Female：Not clever in reading books

读经书不俐
Not smart in reading classics

寅时什么时
What time is Yin?

哥讲给我听
Would you please tell me?

男： 寅时是虎时
Male： Yin is the Period of Tiger

高山上隐居
Live solitarily in the mount

细雨蒙蒙下
Drizzle keeps falling down

进家抓母猪
Break in and take sows away

女： 读诗书不伶
Female：Not clever in reading books

读经书不俐
Not smart in reading classics

卯时什么时
What time is Mao?

哥讲给我听
Would you please tell me?

男： 卯时是兔时[82]
Male： Mao is the period of Rabbit

沿路忙吃草
Eating grass along roads

它虽没刀斧
Without any sword or axe

窝却有多处
Several nests they have built

女： 读诗书不伶
Female： Not clever in reading books

读经书不俐
Not smart in reading classics

辰时什么时
What time is Chen?

哥讲给我听
Would you please tell me?

男： 辰时是龙时
Male： Chen is the Period of Dragon

绞曲下大海
Deep in the sea dragons stay

头架在隆安
His head is in Long'an County

尾扫全天下
While his tail is sweeping free

女：　读诗书不伶
Female：Not clever in reading books

读经书不俐
Not smart in reading classics

巳时什么时
What time is Si?

哥讲给我听
Would you please tell me?

男：　巳时是蛇时
Male：Si is the Period of Snake

匍匐在地边
On the ground it crawls

脖一伸一挺
With neck stretching and shrinking

吓死都是蛙
Worry to death are the frogs

女： 读诗书不伶

Female： Not clever in reading books

读经书不俐

Not smart in reading classics

午时什么时

What time is Wu?

哥讲给我听

Would you please tell me?

男： 午时是马时

Male： Wu is the Period of Horse

日日奔京城

Rush to capital day and night

人以为是飞

As swiftly as it can

四蹄不沾地

Hoofs not touching land as it flies fly

女： 读诗书不伶

Female： Not clever in reading books

读经书不俐

Not smart in reading classics

未时什么时

What time is Wei?

哥讲给我听
Would you please tell me?

男： 未时是羊时
Male： Wei is the Period of Goat

进园吃树叶
Eating leaves in the garden

牵去作祭品
To be taken as sacrifice

哭似儿离娘
Crying as son leaves mom

女： 读诗书不伶
Female： Not clever in reading books

读经书不俐
Not smart in reading classics

申时什么时
What time is Shen?

哥讲给我听
Would you please tell me?

男： 申时是猴时
Male： Shen is the Period of Monkey

嬉戏果树上
On trees enjoying and playing

嘴挑红的吃

It eats the red fruit

眼又望熟的

Looking at the ripe one

女： 读诗书不伶

Female： Not clever in reading books

读经书不俐

Not smart in reading classics

酉时什么时

What time is You?

哥讲给我听

Would you please tell me?

男： 酉时是鸡时

Male： You is the Period of Rooster

捡吃落地米

On the ground pecking rice

尖嘴啄虫豸

Pecking insects with sharp beaks

利眼盯鹰鹞

On hawks they keep a sharp eye

女： 读诗书不伶

Female： Not clever in reading books

读经书不俐
Not smart in reading classics

戌时什么时
What time is Xu?

哥讲给我听
Would you please tell me?

男： 戌时是狗时
Male： Xu is the Period of Dog

日夜守咱家
Watch our house day and night

喂饭它就吃
Eating whatever it's fed

人来它就吠
Barking whenever people approach

女： 读诗书不伶
Female： Not clever in reading books

读经书不俐
Not smart in reading classics

亥时什么时
What time is Hai?

哥讲给我听
Would you please tell me?

男： 亥时是猪时
Male： Hai is the Period of Pig

一窝九兄弟
Nine brothers in a litter

打醮⁸³祭神日
Honoring gods day it comes

用它作供品
Offered as sacrifices to gods

女： 时歌到此止
Female： Here ends the song of hours

辰歌到此完
To end the song of hours

此时完时歌
Let's stop here and go on

再对水旱歌
To sing songs of floods and droughts

水旱 Floods and Droughts

男： 天旱第一年
Male： The first year of drought

一天晴到晚
Fine it is day and night

荫处找不到
No shade'd be found

凉处找不着
Nor a sheltered place

女： 雨顺头一年
Female： In the first year it rains

养鸭又养鹅
Folks raise ducks and geese

养鹅在楼下
Downstairs the geese are raised

公抱孙去看
Grandpa takes his grandson to see

男： 天旱第二年
Male： In the second year of drought

四处各不同
Everywhere is different from others

看东边太阳
The sun rises in the east

太阳红似血
It's as red as blood

女： 雨顺第二年
Female： In the second year of rain

攒钱买田地
Money is saved for buying land

买大田几丘
Several big pieces land we'd buy

租佃给别人
Rent out to others for farming

男： 天旱第三年
Male： In the third year of drought

禾苗全枯萎
All seedlings have withered

枯萎在田里
All have withered in the fields

拿什么养命
How to survive and what to sustain life?

女： 雨顺第三年
Female： In the third year of rain

修仓又打柜
Barns are built and cupboard made

打柜装糙米
Cupboards built for storing brown rice

修仓存稻谷
Barns built for storing rice

男： 天旱第四年
Male： In the fourth year of drought

白播旱禾种
Sowing rice seeds in vain

有塘边田人
Folks with fields beside pond

种块把养命
Do farm work to survive

女： 雨顺第四年
Female： In the fourth year of rain

福气在我家
Good luck stays at my home

傍晚晚饭后
After dinner we stay at home

箫笛齐吹奏
Panpipe and flute we'd play

男： 天旱第五年
Male： In the fifth year of drought

老天杀穷人
The poor are abandoned by Heaven

老天向富人
The rich are blessed by Heaven

推穷人下河
Not care about the poor at all

女： 雨顺第五年
Female： In the fifth year of rain

都出去催债
Out to collect the debts

把债全收齐
All the debts are collected

留过年使用
Reserved for the coming year

男： 天旱第六年
Male： In the sixth year of drought

连竹也枯死

The bamboo has died dry

牛也全死光

Cattle have died all out

让咱怎么办

How to survive and sustain our life?

女： 雨顺第六年

Female： In the sixth year of rain

连下几月雨

Rain keeps falling for month

天天雨哗哗

It rains hard day and night

洪水将淹天

The world'll be covered by flood

男： 天旱第七年

Male： In the seventh year of drought

早晚喝清水

Dringking water day and night

泪水落嘀哒

Tears keep falling down

哪时见这般

Never have I suffered from such drought

女：　雨顺第七年
Female：In the seventh year of rain

咱去催租粮
Folks're asked to give rent rice

租粮收得多
More rent rice is collected

多顾人来运
More hands needed in delivering it

男：　天旱第八年
Male：　In the eighth year of drought

饿殍遍田野
The dead bodies of the starved in the fields

今年什么年
What's the year this year?

全都去逃荒
To escape famine all are out

女：　雨顺第八年
Female：In the eighth year of rain

八兄弟请匠
Together eight brothers hire a craftsman

请来南宁匠
The craftsman is from Nanning

起高楼像宫

Build a house as big as state a government

男： 天旱第九年
Male： In the ninth year of drought

弃府田不耕

Leaving official lands unploughed

弃官田不种

Leaving official lands unsown

扛扁担做贩

Being a vendor with a bamboo pole

女： 雨顺第九年
Female： In the ninth year of rain

下府去催债

Go in for debt collection

把债催回还

Once the debts are paid

过年就安逸

New year will be at ease

男： 天旱第十年
Male： In the tenth year of drought

凑钱买猪鸡

Pigs and chicken we buy

拿去祭雷王

Honor Thunder King as sacrifices

他还不还雨

Will He return with rains?

女： 雨顺第十年

Female： In the tenth year of rain

凑钱去买土

We save money to buy earth

买土来打砖

Buy earth to make bricks

咱起新砖房

New brick house we'd build

注　释

1　Songs 和 Poems 都指代"歌"。Song 指的是歌曲和歌唱；Poem 指的是诗、诗篇、韵文、富有诗意的东西，诗一样的作品，诗一般的事物，美丽的东西或者诗体文。Songs 是指较自由的诗，不刻意讲求对仗、押韵，它可根据歌师需要，尽情地抒发感情，讴歌生活；而 Poems 主要指律诗和排律，它们在字数、句式、格律、押韵上要求较高。

2　Fwen va 为壮语发音，意为唱花。

3　鳄鱼的壮语发音是 ngieng，在壮族民间神话中的意象是可变形的水中怪物，可根据具体情形变幻成猪、鸡、蛇、龙，青年男子或青年女子等不同的形状（陆莲枝，2016）。英文中没有一个单词可以对等表达这个壮语词汇的文化内涵，所以在具体嘹歌文化英译中，本书采取用壮语 ngieng 来将这个句子译为 The ngieng summon the wind，然后以注释的形式予以说明，这样的改写既可以原汁原味地保留壮族文化特色，又不至于在英译中缺省源语文化的精华。通过这个词的英译改写，使壮族文化自信在壮族嘹歌英译中得以体现，传递原生态嘹歌最本真的特色。

4　此处为壮语发音，壮族男子称呼他喜欢的姑娘为"阿妹"（dahnuengx），而姑娘称呼她喜欢的男子为"阿哥"（daeggo），所以此处应该译为 Daeggo。

5　此处同注释 4，壮族青年男女通常以情哥和情妹称呼自己心仪的对象，壮语用阿妹 dahnuengx，阿哥 daeggo 来表达。

6　嘹歌传唱在广西六个市县，亚热带地区的春天气候温暖湿润，南瓜常常种植在农家的田间地头屋旁，南瓜花开鲜嫩大朵，是壮族人民喜爱的入馔食品。

7　亚热带农村田野山坡地区春天多见马蜂，它们辛勤忙碌于采蜜酿蜜，又凶猛勇敢，是壮族人民喜爱的昆虫。

8　亚热带地区春来早，早春三月已是春耕大忙的景象，农村家家户户都利用空地种植自家食用的瓜菜，出门可见各种各样的瓜类，如冬瓜、葫芦瓜、黄瓜、茄瓜等等。此处是比喻用法，形容姑娘心目中的阿哥强壮结实像新生长的瓜。

9　上文用壮语的"阿哥"和"阿妹"来表达人物关系，此处为避免较近距离对唱唱词的重复，而改用汉语"我"和"你"来表达相同的含义。

10　这里用 she 指唱歌者本人，是用第三人称的形式指代自己，表达了壮族姑娘想要表达心意但又害羞掩饰的矛盾心理。

11　此处为嘹歌女方复沓的方式，壮族嘹歌中大量使用女方复沓这种修辞方法。这种格式的歌词容易记忆和传唱，男女问答对唱中大量使用复沓的修辞手法来逗趣唱和。如本书中第 23 首男子唱道："二三月里花满坡，花放枝头娇艳多，花在枝上迎风立，哪个山坡出对歌？"女子唱和道："二三月里花满坡，花放枝头娇艳多，花在树顶临风立，模圩歌圩出对歌。"这里复沓的交叉使用使嘹歌歌词内容妙趣横生，男女唱和对答如流又充满交互的机锋。

12　汉语修辞作为汉文化的重要组成部分，其应用通常与汉文化、汉文化思维、汉民族的文化心理等因素息息相关。在将壮族嘹歌歌词中的汉语修辞方法翻译成英文的具体实践中，源语文化里壮族嘹歌大量运用比喻、借喻、拟人、排比、对仗、重叠、复沓等修辞手法。例如在本书中有许多比喻的修辞法出现，"初见情妹初见人，好比狮子遇麒麟，柚子落到筛子上，碰在一起有圆（缘）分"，这一段用狮子遇麒麟比喻壮族阿哥遇上他心爱的阿妹，用柚子和筛子比喻两人相遇。

13　此处使用 need 的原因一是为了英文表达押韵，此段唱词采用 AABA 的韵式，一二四句末押［iː］韵；二是唱嘹歌是壮族人民生命中不可或缺的重要组成部分，他们每天都要唱嘹歌，欢喜也唱，悲伤也唱，这是他们必不可少的文化瑰宝。

14　壮族人称柚子树叶为"菩叶"，所以英文用 Pomelo 来表达。

15　再不找冬衣，指的是再不准备冬天的衣服，很快就要挨冷受冻，而且亚热带的冬天短暂，一两个月就会过去。壮族人朴实内敛，他们用日常所见的天气、植物、农活等主题表达内心淳朴的爱情，这里形容壮族阿哥爱慕自己的姑娘想表白又犹豫，担心时光飞逝的矛盾心理。

16　Gu(x)是菰花的壮语发音。

17　Baem(h)是萠花的壮语发音。

18　Ra(q)是楠树的壮语发音。

19　Haw Mo(z)是莫圩的壮语发音。

20　Va vengj 是枉花的壮语发音。

21　Va mai 是黄花的壮语发音。

22　The Han's 是蔗园地的壮语发音。蔗园地是亚热带产糖植物甘蔗的种植园地。

23　此句译文采用目前英美国家主流社会也认可的中式英文表达"人山人海"，来形容唱歌阿妹心中既急切地想去歌圩见到阿哥，又矜持地表达虽然歌圩有很多姑娘前往，她也不急于赶去的心理。

24　此处形容壮族阿妹口是心非的矛盾心理，虽然心里倾慕着阿哥，但是嘴上却不肯承认，毕竟爱在心头口难开。在壮族传统里，示爱应该是男子汉要做的事情。

25　壮族阿妹的这句唱词意指她已心有所属，虽然歌圩上青年小伙子到处都是，他们都亮丽地在眼前经过，但是谁也没有阿妹心目中看上的阿哥那么帅。英文这样译，取自一首脍炙人口的英文歌 Take Me to Your Heart（《吻别》）中的唱词："So many people all around the world. Tell me where do I find someone like you girl"（世界上有很多人，告诉我在哪里可以找到像你这样的女孩?）。这样以英语世界广为流传的英文歌曲唱词，使得嘹歌英语译文的读者受众更易理解嘹歌中壮族姑娘看上了她心目中阿哥的心理描绘。

26　此处将"哥"译为 lover 而不是 brother，一是因为避免重复改用称呼，二是《三月歌》的嘹歌唱到此处，青年男女的感情已经渐入佳境，彼此情投意合，逐渐愿意表达互为倾慕的情愫，所以阿妹的唱词已转为更肯定中意情郎的地步。

27　男女这段唱词中的"同"是两个意思，一个是一起的意思；一个是老同、老庚的意思，壮族最好的朋友会结成老同。这里的同是老同，男老同叫公同，女老同叫娅同。"同真想去拔"是老同真想过去拔的意思。"同慢过去拔"则是老同慢慢过去拔的意思。

28　这里的"菜花"指的是雪里蕻。

29　壮族年轻姑娘不一定插花在鬓角，也有插在头上或发尾的。

30　这里的插花是种花，地府不是府第，而是地方、土地的意思。所以整句的意思是：跟人家一起出去种花，种花会占地方。

31　"去恋"是去交友去谈恋爱的意思。整句的意思是：我们交友谈恋爱谈得过别人,我们才高兴才舒服。这里的谈过别人有另一层意思,就是谈得过对方的旧情人。

32 "插筒"的意思是竹筒。现代有花盆,古代只能用竹筒。插在筒里就像现在的一盆花,可以送给对方当礼物。

33 Tung 是桐花的壮语发音。

34 Lim(z)是苓花的壮语发音。

35 枉树是金樱树,因此译为 Golden Blossom。

36 *El Condor Pasa*(老鹰之歌)是南美秘鲁一带一首反抗西班牙殖民者的印地安民歌,后被 Paul Simon(保罗·西蒙)重唱组改编,用英文翻唱,风行全球,成为南美洲最具代表性的一首民谣,这首旋律已经被列入联合国世界文化遗产。此处英文是模仿这首歌曲里反复出现的歌词:I'd rather be a sparrow than a snail, I'd rather be a hammer than a nail,以期令英语世界的受众更易理解体会其中深意。

37 Dok 是柠树的壮语发音。

38 Vanj leaves 是菀菜的壮语音译。

39 Gosa 是纱树的壮语,叶子可用来喂猪,树皮可以用来做土砂纸,汉语也称为构树。

40 Mbonq 是苈菜的壮文发音。

41 壮语的"臭青"原来指的是青菜煮不熟而带有的让人不悦的一股味道,此处延伸意义为餐餐都吃苈菜,都产生味觉审美疲劳了,一闻到苈菜的味道就倒胃口。

42 壮语中"满崽"指的是最小那个孩子,相当于汉语的"幺儿"。

43 红蓝叶是一种做五色糯米饭的植物染料,汉语叫作蓝靛,壮语叫作 Gyaemq。这里指的是壮族人用来做糯米饭的染料,有红、紫两种颜色,文中的紫色就是蓝,红蓝就是紫色的和红色的。

44 红草紫叶的壮语是 Ci(j) and Se,这里是壮语英译。

45 Steaming rice 是指蒸糯米饭,农历三月三是壮族一个重大的节庆日,家家户户都做五色糯米饭。

46 这段男子的唱词第二、三句,形容到了农历三月三,家家闹哄哄,喧闹得像州府、衙门,就像现在的县府、省府。

47 壮族把在自己房子后面的房子叫上房、上屋;自己房子前面的叫下房、下屋。在这里,爹、爸爸指的是父辈的人;下一段女唱词中出现的伯、伯母伯父指的是比父辈大的人,都是泛指。

48　因为在中国古代通过科举考试是做官的主要途径,"跟"在壮语中是"与"
　　"和"的意思。

49　壮族男女对唱嗷歌,一般是按照时间日期顺序来进行的,上句男子领唱句
　　末唱他打算"初三日扫墓",接下来女子应和末句是她打算"初五日扫墓"。
　　男女唱完扫墓这一回合,继续按时间顺序进行对唱,所以会出现在新唱
　　段,男子领衔从"三月初四"又接着唱的情形。

50　此处的"肥料"与我们通常理解的施肥肥料不是同一种物质,此处指的是
　　家里有很多菜肴的人家。

51　"二三月"指的是农历,全书均为农历,统一在此处注释中说明。

52　壮族有在农历二月份春分(即阳历三月份)和农历三月份清明(即阳历四
　　月份)给家族故人扫墓祭奠的传统,所以这句唱词是说农历二三月扫墓。

53　Hanq hag 是一种名叫"寒哈"的鸟的壮文音译,这种鸟鸣叫声清脆动人。

54　轭是指套在牲口脖子上弯曲的木材,这种树木适合做牛轭。这段唱词意
　　思是男子自己说家贫,没有钱买牛,也没有钱买牛轭,他家做牛轭的木头
　　现在还长在树上。

55　"外家"在壮语里指的是丈夫父母的家,所以英文用 parents-in-law 来表
　　达,此处英文出于押韵考虑为简写。

56　壮语的"家公"和"家婆"指的是"外公""外婆"。

57　此处指的是家里没有钱买壮牛耕田,只能把小牛和老牛都派上用场去耕
　　耘。老牛步履蹒跚脚步沉重,遇到田埂时,人得从牛后面放下扛着的犁
　　耙,走到牛前面拉它走上田埂,极言劳作辛苦、生活不易。

58　此处为一男一女对唱,他俩都在通过唱词试探对方的婚姻状况,以便了解
　　是否男未娶、女未嫁。

59　此处的"友"指朋友,英文中未体现,因为是男子唱给女子听,所以不需要
　　赘述。

60　此处指的是稻谷成熟了,男子邀请女子来帮忙收稻谷。

61　"典仓粮"指的是晚稻刚抽穗,还没有结新米,回家清理粮仓旧米以备不时
　　之需。

62　"开旧粮"指的是新米未出,青黄不接的时候,回家打开粮仓清点旧货。

63　"二两油"中的"二"是中文特有的虚数,英文用 some 来表示"一些",属于
　　不确定的数字。

64　The Day 大写,特指农历七月十四日是壮族的鬼节,要办仪式来祭奠鬼
　　神,以求来年风调雨顺、家泰人安。

65 壮语里"成根"指的是开枝散叶,祝福一个人子孙满堂。

66 壮语中的"挦"指的是打谷子,这句意为丈夫打谷子,妻子来炒米。

67 壮语里"妖精"指的是男子的妻子很精明,懂得别出心裁地耗费鸡油来炒香新谷。

68 爨(cuàn)指的是烧火做饭(cook)。"爨,炊也。"出自《广雅》。取其进火谓之爨,取其气上谓之炊。这句唱词指的是与姑母分灶台开火,各吃各的,不一起吃饭的意思。

69 在壮族农村,生活还不富裕时,农户只有过年才会把辛辛苦苦饲养了一年的猪拿来宰杀以备过节。

70 如前所述,壮语里老同指的是好朋友。此句是男子佯装嗔怨女子到了寒冬腊月有新被子御寒,而不顾他的寒暖。

71 中文的"晦"是指农历每月的最后一天,即大月三十日、小月二十九日。正月晦日作为一年的第一晦日即"初晦",受到古人的重视,寄托了古代中国劳动人民祛邪、避灾、祈福的美好愿望。

72 壮族嘹歌歌圩一般都设置在平缓的土坡、田间地头或者露天场地,壮族嘹歌歌圩通常译为 Liao Songs Fair。

73 壮族大粽子被当作过年必备的好物,这句指的是吃了大粽子身体才能吸收好营养,从而有力气干活。

74 黄花对应的是用于染黄色糯米饭的染料植物。

75 当地壮人称操汉语粤方言的汉人为"客人",称操汉语北方方言的汉人为"军人"。

76 此处中文省略,英文为完整表达。

77 蚰蜒是一种惊蛰时分最早鸣叫的昆虫,壮语音译为 gveng gveiq。

78 "妹"在中文句末是称呼对方的意思。

79 "同"在中文句末是称呼对方为老同的意思。

80 一月在此指的是十一月。

81 中文这句原义是"十一月是建子月",英文表达与中文对应。"哥"在中文句末是称呼对方的意思。

82 壮族用动物对应十二时辰。

83 此句的原义是"养它来做肉",在此译为"用它做贡品"。

后 记

　　嘹歌产生并流传于广西壮族自治区的平果、田东、田阳、德保、马山、武鸣等六个县市，是壮族先民留给后人的宝贵精神财富，是壮族原生态文化的百科全书，是世世代代壮族人民奉献给祖国文化宝库的人类口头和非物质文化遗产。英译壮族优秀传统文化对于做好少数民族地区文化建设、增加民族身份认同感、维护边疆地区稳定、增强国家文化软实力、推进负责任的大国形象对外传播至关重要。嘹歌作为承载壮族传统精神文化的历史记录，被列入国家级非物质文化遗产名录，具有重要的民族文化价值和学术研究价值。系统地整理、翻译和出版壮族嘹歌典籍，使珍贵而优秀的壮族文化走向世界，具有深远的意义和影响。本书是由中国社会科学院民族文学研究所从事中国南方民族文学研究的罗汉田先生进行的壮文转写和汉文翻译，由 2004 年被平果县人民政府授予"嘹歌歌师"称号的平果县太平镇太平村布凌屯壮族农民谭绍明歌师提供歌书抄本。

　　我对壮族嘹歌的关注得从我的美国访学经历谈起。2015 年至 2017 年，我作为纽约州立大学人类学系的高级访问学者经常参加纽约写作协会举办的学术交流活动。该协会定期举办主题报告会，与会学者们可以在会上分享不同国家和民族的文学和文化作品。有一期主题是非物质文化遗产，我想借此机会，有选择性地介绍一下广西被列入国家级非物质文化遗产代表性项目名录的非遗项目，便先后介绍了广西的花山岩画和壮族嘹歌。壮族嘹歌于 2008 年经国务院批准，入选第二批国家级非物质文化遗产代表性项目名录。嘹歌的诗性语言、旋律唱调都很美，作品的内容题材和审美功能、教化功能也都是积极的、正面的，都带有引人向善的意义。纽约是一座世界级的文化中心城市，那里经常会举办一些带有世界影响力的文化艺术活动，例如国际纪录片双年展等。来自世界各地不同国家的艺术家和学者都想通过这些平台将自己国家独有的优秀传统文化展示给世界。我深知,作为一个来自广西壮乡的学者,既然有机会来到纽约这座城市,就应该为讲好广西故事,乃至中国故事做点力所能及的事。那个时候的我就萌生了从事壮族嘹歌英译、向世界推介广西壮族优秀传统文化嘹歌的强烈念头。

壮族,是一个逢事必唱、无处不歌的民族。华南珠江流域、东南亚、环太平洋地区那文化带、铜鼓、花山、布洛陀、山歌、嘹歌、歌圩……时空经纬撑起这片壮民族文化体系。2017年下半年回国后,广西这片古老神秘的土地,壮族这个勤劳朴实的民族,花山岩画上的小红人、征战的铜鼓声声、歌咏生产生活的嘹歌,常常出现在我的梦里挥之不去。2018年,我收到了罗汉田老师转写的壮汉双语嘹歌五部长歌——《三月歌》《贼歌》《行路歌》《日歌》《房屋歌》和一部短歌《浪花歌》系列丛书,被他努力挖掘壮民族元素的拳拳之心和严谨求实的科研精神深深打动。罗老师授权交给我进行英译《三月歌》,这一本三千多行五言四句的歌唱四季赏花农事春忙爱情。2021年4月25日上交22万字的《三月歌》英译稿后,罗老师把余下四部作品都授权给了我。这些日子以来接触到壮族嘹歌保护传承的前辈们都很大力支持我的工作,使我觉得很温暖,他们是:中央民族大学原副校长梁庭望教授、中国社会科学院研究员罗汉田研究员、广西壮学会覃乃昌会长、平果人大主任农敏坚、嘹歌会长和壮族土俗字传承人黄国观、嘹歌传承人陆顺红、歌圩传承人黄富家,以及平果文体广旅局莫掩策主任。此外,我还要感谢平果市政府帮忙精准对接嘹歌歌师和传承人。

2021年4月,我与广西社会科学院文史研究所李萍副所长一起去参加平果市耶圩镇的嘹歌歌圩,她的博士论文题目是《壮族嘹歌文化的现代重构》。我们一起深入镇上歌圩,采访了当地嘹歌歌师。在全球化、现代化和城市化的滔天巨浪中,目不识丁、临机自撰、连唱几天几夜不歇的嘹歌手已为数不多,已经成为他们日常生产生活生命中重要组成部分的嘹歌更像是他们的精神支柱。我们在田间地头的嘹歌歌圩陶醉地听歌者唱了四十分钟,不自觉地把歌声和几年来英译的《三月歌》联系起来,我不禁感叹在如今这个快节奏的时代,这样的两两对唱是多么富有诗情画意——以嘹歌的方式娓娓道来浅唱低吟,真实地呈现了壮族人内敛又奔放的民族特性。

艰苦而富于启发性的平果嘹歌歌圩田野调查的日子忙碌而充实,传统嘹歌形式和与时俱进的内容不断创新,新译本更注重接受度调查。我们奔赴平果县果化镇永定村,参观乡贤农敏坚个人斥资60万元兴建的书、歌、节三位一体嘹歌博物馆。农敏坚先生做过县长、县委书记和人大常委主任,他在任内推广了那坡黑衣壮和平果嘹歌,文化不是吹糠见米的事情,他却不遗余力地为家乡人民留下一份宝贵的精神财富。在博物馆,农敏坚先生打电话来说一定要赠予我两套嘹歌系列丛书,令我倍感温暖。平果市电视台副台长余执老师是我的壮语老师,他是著名的壮语作家,1986 年开始发表壮语作品,至今已著有小说 200 篇,散文 100 篇,山歌 50 篇。他带我们观看了欢嘹乐队的嘹歌演出。余执老师的夫人梁洲利是这个女子嘹歌乐队的主唱,她领唱的嘹歌歌声如同天籁,极富穿透力,她们把哈嘹、那海嘹、斯格嘹、底格嘹、长嘹、哟伊嘹组成嘹歌串烧。霎时间,那带着壮族稻谷秧苗田野的气息扑面而来,悠悠的清唱没有任何伴奏,却给人以绝美的艺术享受。

我在平果市嘹歌传承人陆顺红会长的嘹歌培训中心与平果文联主席梁颖武谈非遗嘹歌的保护、传承和再发展,梁主席如数家珍地介绍目前平果嘹歌的三大流派:原生态派、新嘹歌派和创新派,以及它们各自的特色。我在平果文广旅局访谈壮族嘹歌协会黄国观会长时,作为壮族土俗字传承人的他亮出嘹歌土俗字手抄本,壮族人对土俗字也就是古壮字有感情,拉丁壮文是官方推广的文字,是人民币纸币的五种少数民族语言之一,是族群认同的标志。黄会长不仅是嘹歌歌王,还以嘹歌为载体,创作了不同题材的相关作品,把冗长抽象的官方文件化作人们喜闻乐见的嘹歌,真正做到了传统嘹歌与时俱进地现代转型。

我曾有幸在平果歌圩现场看到壮族嘹歌的对唱,这是一个好客又质朴,开放又保守的民族,以歌会友以歌传情,唱党百年华诞,唱爱情友情禁毒国安,内容与时俱进;文唱是临机自撰,机锋交互,对唱是根据歌本你来我往再用高低音搭配交互出不同的音效和气氛;嘹歌是两男两女对歌,据说这样男女不单独接触,不会违背男女之大防,另一对则充当电灯泡的作用;男子口袋装几本歌书有备而来,女子根据男唱对答如流,就像刘三姐智胜歌书装满船而来的三秀才,看来女子在语言和音乐表达上还是略胜一筹。农历三月十五歌圩是村里一个盛大的节日,乡规民约这一天出门对歌开门迎客,家境殷实的大户杀猪宰羊大宴宾客,哪一家来客多就预示着来年丰收兴旺。在嘹歌协会黄有加会长家吃饭,他老伴喜笑颜开地端上来一盆又一盆的佳肴,鸡鸭猪羊应有尽有,仿佛我们要是全部吃完,她家明天的筵席更丰盛,这种真诚和热情令人难以忘怀和回报。步行前去耶圩镇歌圩的路上,偶遇陆顺红会长,这个长得英挺帅气的平果嘹歌会长,一路陪同我们深入林中歌圩,他真是平果嘹歌的代言人,热爱嘹歌,德高望重,不仅热情地与圩上歌友招呼致意,还歌技高超地飙高音配合他的男伴制造现场气氛,带动了他们这个嘹歌二人组。唯热爱和真情实感动人,他俊朗的脸庞也激动的红着,58 岁看上去仿佛是一个少年,陌上公子翩翩来,裤子口袋里还装有两本歌书。在嘹歌培训中心,他热情地招呼老师们教我唱嘹歌,仿佛我要是学不会唱一首嘹歌就不能进行访谈的样子。他对嘹歌的热爱由内而外自然流露。

莫掩策是平果文广旅局办公室主任,他还有一个身份是享誉国内外的哈嘹乐队主创,平果嘹歌总设计师农敏坚先生当年担任县领导职务时爱才惜才,把当年在平果铝厂做工人,且酷爱唱嘹歌的莫掩策纳入麾下,在文化馆专职研习嘹歌并逐渐转型为嘹歌的管理人员。在耶圩镇嘹歌歌圩,他演唱了思念歌《山中画眉》,舒缓的嘹歌与现代摇滚元素混搭,华南珠江流域的壮族汉子,深情细腻,质朴内敛,现场美的感受无与伦比。传统的壮族嘹歌有五部长歌一部短歌,现在出现很多应景的创新作品,传统嘹歌在中国共产党领导下的社会主义新农村发挥着新时代兼具审美和教化功能的巨大作用。

将近四年翻译《平果壮族嘹歌——三月歌篇》的过程非常艰难。用壮汉语记录的壮族嘹歌面临跨文化传播交流中的翻译问题,几经翻译实践和翻译理论学习摸索,这一本书采用罗选民教授 2016 年首次提出的"大翻译"观,即倡导宏观性语符翻译和跨学科翻译研究,将翻译置于语言、文化、跨学科等层面加以审视,是统观之下的语符翻译。嘹歌是著名的壮族长篇古歌,经过口头传诵再通过文人用古壮字记录形成歌谣集,是壮族人民世代相传的集体文化记忆。为此,译者应该了解源语和目标语语言/符号翻译所涉及的各种因素,采用阐释、改写和适应等翻译技术手段,对嘹歌这一非物质文化遗产和民间文艺进行创造性转化和创新性发展,确保壮族嘹歌高质量的译介和对外传播。在讲好广西故事,对外推介广西壮族嘹歌这项非物质文化遗产的翻译实践中,从目标语读者和受众的接受度角度考量,文化翻译责无旁贷,只有有意识地从文化层面、语言层面和跨学科层面对这个问题加以认真研究落实,才能确保优秀的壮族文化得以成功地翻译推广到国际舞台。在优秀中华文化"走出去"的浪潮中,需要用文化翻译的方法对壮族嘹歌进行汉英翻译,以确保这份壮族民间文艺瑰宝得以保持本真性以及高质量的译介和对外传播。

自我在美国纽约州立大学人类学系做高级访问学者,并开始从事广西非物质文化遗产项目推介工作以来,已经走过七年多的历程,在理论和实践上都积累了扎实的基础。在壮族嘹歌英译和对外传播方面,协助制作了音视频和纪录片;发表了相关的中英文论文三篇;即将出版英译平果壮族嘹歌系列作品。在"中华文化走出去""讲好中国故事""新国际传播"的国家战略发展形势下,我一直致力于英译对外宣传壮族嘹歌,通过提升中华文化、中国故事的国际传播能力，充分服务国家战略发展的需要，进而为建构中国国际话语体系，增强中国文化软实力做出中国外语人的应有贡献。为此，我将继续深挖广西十二个世居少数民族优秀的传统文化，以英语世界受众可接受度恰当的方式，为当前时期让世界了解一个真实的中国和真实的广西做出贡献，为新时代讲好广西故事添砖加瓦。

是为后记。

陈　兵

撰于广西大学东校园